"RENDELL IS AWFULLY GOOD . . . IN ANY RENDELL BOOK YOU KNOW THAT SOMETHING UNUSUAL IS GOING TO HAPPEN."

The New York Times Book Review

"When Rendell writes crime-from-the-criminal-point-of-view, she is gripping and creepy. When she writes straightforward detection starring homely, countryish Inspector Wexford, she is even better. Only P. D. James can rival Rendell for total, no-seams-showing command of the classic genre, and true mystery fans, unlike literary critics, would probably give Rendell extra points for unliterary economy and ease of her irresistible non-stop prose."

The Kirkus Reviews

The
Secret House
of Death

Ruth Rendell

BALLANTINE BOOKS • NEW YORK

All rights reserved. Published in the United States by Ballantine Books, a division of Random House, Inc., New York.

ISBN 0-345-29282-0

This edition published by arrangement with Doubleday & Company, Inc.

Manufactured in the United States of America

First Ballantine Books Edition: October 1970
Third printing: October 1980

For Douglas Blass

Then is it sin
To rush into the secret house of death
Ere death dare come to us?
Antony and Cleopatra

Chapter One

The man was heavily built and he drove a big car, a green Ford Zephyr. This was his third visit to the house called Braeside in Orchard Drive, Matchdown Park, and each time he parked his car on the grass patch in the pavement. He was in his early thirties, dark and not bad-looking. He carried a briefcase. He never stayed very long but Louise North who lived at Braeside with her husband Bob was always pleased to see him and admitted him with a smile.

These were facts and by now everyone who lived in the vicinity was aware of them. The Airedale who lived opposite and who belonged to some people called Winter obligingly kept them informed of the big man's visits. At day-long sentry-go behind his gate, the Airedale barked at strangers, kept silence for residents. He barked furiously now as the man strolled up the Norths' path, knocked at the front door, and, thirty seconds later after a whispered word with Louise, disappeared inside. His duty done, the dog nosed out a brown earth-encrusted bone and began to gnaw it. One by one the women his outburst had alerted retreated from their windows and considered what they had seen.

The ground had been prepared, the seed sown. Now all that remained was for these enthusiastic gardeners to raise their crop of gossip and take it to market over the fences and over the tea-cups.

Of them all only Susan Townsend, who lived next door to Braeside, wanted to be left out of this exchange of merchandise. She sat typing each afternoon in her window and was no more proof than they were against raising her eyes when the dog barked. She wondered about the man's visits but, unlike her neighbours, she felt no lubricious curiosity. Her own husband had walked out on her just a year ago and the man's visits to Louise North touched chords of pain she hoped had begun to atrophy. Adultery, which excites and titillates the innocent, had brought her at twenty-six into a dismal abyss of loneliness. Let her neighbours speculate as to why the man came, what Louise wanted, what Bob thought, what would come of it all. From personal experience she knew the answers and all she wanted was to get on with her work, bring up her son and not get herself involved.

The man left forty minutes later and the Airedale barked again. He stopped abruptly as his owner approached and, standing on his hind legs—in which position he wriggled like a belly dancer—fawned on the two little boys she had fetched from school.

Susan Townsend went into her kitchen and put the kettle on. The side gate banged.

'Sorry we're so late, my dear,' said Doris Winter, stripping off her gloves and homing on the nearest radiator. 'But your Paul couldn't find his cap and we've been rooting through about fifty lockers.'

'Roger Gibbs had thrown it into the junior playground.' said Susan's son virtuously. 'Can I have a biscuit?'

'You may not. You'll spoil your tea.'

'Can Richard stay?'

It is impossible to refuse such a request when the putative guest's mother is at your elbow. 'Of course,' said Susan. 'Go and wash your hands.'

'I'm frozen,' Doris said. 'Winter by name and Winter by nature, that's me.' It was March and mild, but Doris was always cold, always huddled under layers of sweaters and cardigans and scarves. She divested herself gradually of her outer coverings, kicked off her shoes and pressed chilblained feet against the radiator. 'You don't know how I envy you your central heating. Which brings me to what I wanted to say. Did you see what I saw? Louise's boy-friend paying her yet another visit?'

'You don't know he's her boy-friend, Doris.'

'She says he's come to sell central heating. I asked her—got the cheek of the devil, haven't I?—and that's what she said. But when I mentioned it to Bob you could see he didn't have the least idea what I meant. "We're not having central heating," he said. "I can't afford it." There now. What d'you think of that?'

'It's their business and they'll have to sort it out.'

'Oh, quite. I couldn't agree more. I'm sure I'm not interested in other people's sordid private lives. I do wonder what she sees in this man, though. It's not as if he was all that to write home about and Bob's a real dream. I've always thought him by far the most attractive man around here, all that cool fresh charm.'

'You make him sound like a deodorant,' said Susan, smiling in spite of herself. 'Shall we go in the other room?'

Reluctantly, Doris unpeeled herself from the radiator and, carrying shoes, shedding garments in her wake, followed Susan into the living-room. 'Still, I suppose good looks don't really count,' she went on persistently. 'Human nature's a funny thing. I know that from my nursing days . . .'

Sighing inwardly, Susan sat down. Once on to her nursing days and the multifarious facets of human idiosyncrasy to be observed in a hospital ward, Doris was liable to go on for hours. She listened with half an ear to the inevitable spate of anecdote.

'. . . And that was just one example. It's amazing the people who are married to absolutely marvellous-looking other people and who fall in love with absolute horrors. I suppose they just want a change.'

'I suppose they do,' Susan said evenly.

'But fancy trusting someone and having complete faith in them and then finding they've been deceiving you all along. Carrying on and making a fool of you. Oh, my dear, forgive me! What have I said? I didn't mean you, I was speaking generally, I was—'

'It doesn't matter,' Susan cut in. She was used to tactlessness and it wasn't the tactlessness she minded but the sudden belated awareness on the part of speakers that they had dropped bricks. They insisted on covering up, making excuses and embarking on long disquisitions aimed to show that Susan's was an exceptional case. Doris did this now, giggling nervously and rubbing her still cold hands.

'I mean, of course, Julian *did* carry on behind your back, meeting what's-her-name, Elizabeth, when he was supposed to be working. And you've got a trusting nature like poor Bob. But Julian never did it on his own doorstep, did he? He never brought Elizabeth here.' Doris added transparently, 'I know that for sure. I should have seen.'

'I'm sure you would,' said Susan.

The two little boys came downstairs, their arms full of miniature cars. Susan settled them at the table, hoping Doris would take the hint and go. Perhaps she was over-protective but Paul was, after all, the child of a broken marriage and on her rested the responsibility of seeing he didn't grow up with too jaundiced a view of matrimony. She glanced at Doris now and slightly shook her head.

'Just listen to my dog,' Doris said too brightly. 'It's a wonder the neighbours don't complain.' She trotted to the window, gathering up shed garments as she went, and shook her fist at the Airedale, a gesture which inflamed him to a frenzy. He stuck his big woolly head over the gate and began to howl. 'Be quiet, Pollux!' Susan often wondered why the Airedale had been named after one of the Gemini. Orchard Drive must be thankful the Winters had no Castor to keep him company. 'It's the new baker's roundsman that's set him off this time,' Doris said sagely. 'He never barks at us or you or the Gibbses or the Norths. Which just goes to show it's fear with him and not aggressiveness, whatever people may say.' She glared at her son and said, as if instead of placidly eating bread and butter, he had been urging her to stay, 'Well, I can't hang about here all night, you know. I've got Daddy's dinner to get.'

Susan sat down with the children and ate a sandwich. If you had not 'Daddy's dinner' to get, you certainly prepared none for yourself and tea was a must. Paul crammed a last chocolate biscuit into his mouth and began pushing a diminutive red fire engine across the cloth and over the plates.

'Not at the table, darling.'

Paul scowled at her and Richard, whose hands had been itching to reach for a dumper truck, hid them under the table and gave him a virtuous glance. 'Please may I leave the table, Mrs. Townsend?'

'I suppose so. Your hands aren't sticky, are they?'

But both little boys were on the floor by now, trundling their fleet of vehicles and making realistic if exaggerated engine sounds. They wriggled across the carpet on their stomachs, making for Susan's desk.

This was a Victorian mahogany affair full of niches and cubbyholes. Susan had sufficient empathy to understand its fascination for a five-year-old with a mania for Lilliputian vehicles and she tried to turn a blind eye when Paul used its shelves for garages, her writing paper boxes for ramps and her ribbon tins for turntables. She poured herself a second cup of tea and jumped, slopping it into her saucer, as the paper clip box fell to the floor and fasteners sprayed everywhere. While Richard, the ingratiating guest, scuttled to retrieve them, Paul stuck a jammy hand on Miss Willingale's manuscript and began to use it for a racing track.

'Now that's quite enough,' Susan said crisply. 'Outside both of you till bedtime.'

She washed the tea things and went upstairs. The children had crossed the road and were poking toys at Pollux through the curlicues of the wrought-iron gate. Susan opened the window.

'You're to stay on this side,' she called. 'All the cars will be along in a minute.'

The Airedale wagged his tail and made playful bites at a lorry bonnet Paul had thrust into his face. Susan, who hadn't been thinking about Julian nearly so much lately, suddenly remembered how he used to call Pollux an animated fun fur. This was the time Julian used to come home, the first of the commuting husbands to return. Pollux was still there and unchanged; as usual the children littered the front garden with their toys; the cherry trees were coming into bloom and the first lights of evening appearing in the houses. Only one thing had altered: Julian would never come again. He had always hated Matchdown Park, that detestable dormitory as he called it, and now he had a flat ten minutes from his office in New Bridge Street. He would be walking home now to vent upon Elizabeth his brilliance, his scorn, his eternal fussing over food, his didactic opinions. Elizabeth would have the joy and the excitement—and the fever-pitch exasperation—until the day came when Julian found someone else. Stop it, Susan told herself sternly, stop it.

She began to brush her fair shiny hair—thinner and less glossy since the divorce. Sometimes she wondered why she bothered. There was no one to see her but a little boy and the chance of a friend dropping in was almost nil. Married couples wanted to see other married couples, not a divorcee who hadn't even the advantage of being the guilty and therefore interesting party.

She had hardly seen any of those smart childless friends since the divorce. Minta Philpot had phoned once and cooled when she heard Susan hadn't a man in tow, much less was planning on remarriage. What had become of Lucius and Mary, of lovely remote Dian and her husband Greg? Perhaps Julian saw them, but he was Julian Townsend, the editor of *Certainty*, eternally sought after, eternally a personage.

The children were safely occupied on the lawn by now and the first homing husband had arrived, Martin Gibbs with a bunch of flowers for Betty. That, at any rate, awoke no painful memories. Julian had never been what he called a 'hothouse hubby' and Susan had been lucky to get flowers on her birthday.

And here, exactly on time, was Bob North.

He was tall, dark and exceptionally good-looking. His clothes were unremarkable but he wore them with a grace that seemed unconscious and his masculinity just saved him from looking like a male model. The face was too classically perfect to suit modern cinematic requirements and yet it was not the face of a gigolo, not in the least Italianate. It was an English face, Celtic, clear-skinned and frank.

Susan had lived next door to him and his wife since they had moved to Braeside two years before. But Julian had despised his neighbours, calling them bourgeois, and of them all only Doris had been sufficiently pushing and thick-skinned to thrust her friendship on the Townsends. Susan knew Bob just well enough to justify the casual wave she now gave him from her window.

He waved back with the same degree of amiable indifference, took the ignition key from his car and strolled out on to the pavement. Here he stood for a few seconds gazing at the ruts the green Zephyr had made in the turf. His face had grown faintly troubled but when he turned and glanced upwards, Susan retreated, unwilling to meet his eyes. Herself the victim of a deceiver, she knew how quickly a fellow-feeling for Bob North could grow, but she didn't want to be involved in the Norths' problems. She went downstairs and called Paul in.

When he was in bed, she sat beside him and read the nightly instalment of Beatrix Potter. Strong-featured, flaxen-haired, he was his mother's son, as unlike Julian as could be.

'Now read it all again,' he said as she closed the book.

'You must be joking. It's ten to seven. *Ten to seven.*'

'I like that book, but I don't think a dog would ever go to tea with a cat or take it a bunch of flowers. It's stupid to give people flowers. They only die.' He threw himself about on the bed, laughing scornfully. Perhaps, Susan thought, as she tucked him up again, he wasn't so unlike Julian, after all.

'I tidied up all your papers,' he said, opening one eye. 'I can have my cars on your desk, if I tidy up, can't I?'

'I suppose so. I bet you didn't tidy up the garden.'

Immediately he simulated exhaustion, pulling the bedclothes over his head.

'One good turn deserves another,' Susan said and she went out into the garden to collect the scattered fleet of cars from lawn and flower-beds.

The street was deserted now and dusk was falling. The lamps, each a greenish translucent jewel, came on one by one and the Winters' gate cast across the road a fantastic shadow like lace made by a giant's hand.

Susan was groping for toys in the damp grass when she heard a voice from behind the hedge. 'I think this is your son's property.' Feeling a little absurd—she had been on all-fours—she got up and took the two-inch-long lorry from Bob North's hands.

'Thanks,' she said. 'It would never do to lose this.'

'What is it, anyway?'

'A kind of road sweeper. He had it in his stocking.'

'Good thing I spotted it.'

'Yes, indeed.' She moved away from the fence. This was the longest conversation she had ever had with Bob North and she felt it had been deliberately engineered, that he had come out on purpose to speak to her. Once again he was staring at the ruined turf. She felt for a truck under the lilac bush.

'Mrs. Townsend—er, Susan?'

She sighed to herself. It wasn't that she minded his use of her christian name but that it implied an intimacy he might intend to grow between them. I'm as bad as Julian, she thought.

'Sorry,' she said. 'How rude of me.'

'Not at all. I just wondered . . .' He had dark blue eyes, a smoky marbled blue like lapis, and now he turned them away to avoid hers. 'You do your typing at the window, don't you? Your writing or whatever it is?'

'I do typed copies of manuscripts, yes. But only for

this one novelist.' Of course, he wasn't asking about this aspect of it at all. Anything to deflect him. 'I wouldn't consider . . .'

'I wanted to ask you,' he interrupted, 'if ever . . . Well, if today . . .' His voice trailed away. 'No, forget it.'

'I don't look out of the window much,' Susan lied. She was deeply embarrassed. For perhaps half a minute they confronted each other over the hedge, eyes downcast, not speaking. Susan fidgeted with the little car she was holding and then Bob North said suddenly:

'You're lucky to have your boy. If we, my wife and I . . .'

That doesn't work, Susan almost cried aloud. Children don't keep people together. Don't you read the newspapers? 'I must go in,' she stammered. 'Good night.' She gave him a quick awkward smile. 'Good night, Bob.'

'Good night, Susan.'

So Doris had been right, Susan thought distastefully. There was something and Bob was beginning to guess. He was on the threshold, just where she had been eighteen months ago when Julian, who had always kept strict office hours, started phoning with excuses at five about being late home.

'Elizabeth?' he had said when Susan took that indiscreet phone call. 'Oh, *that* Elizabeth. Just a girl who keeps nagging me to take her dreary cookery features.'

What did Louise say? 'Oh, *that* man. Just a fellow who keeps nagging me to buy central heating.'

Back to Miss Willingale. Paul hadn't exaggerated when he had said he had tidied her desk. It was as neat as a pin, all the paper stacked and the two ballpoint pens put on the left of the typewriter. He had even emptied her ashtray.

Carefully she put all the cars away in their boxes before sitting down. This was the twelfth manuscript she had prepared for Jane Willingale in eight years, each time transforming a huge unwieldy ugly duckling of blotted scribblings into a perfect swan, spotless, clear and neat. Swans they had been indeed. Of the twelve, four had been best sellers, the rest close runners-up. She had worked for Miss Willingale while still Julian's secretary, after her marriage and after Paul was born. There seemed no reason to leave her in the lurch just because she was now divorced. Besides, apart from the satisfaction of doing the job well, the novels afforded her a huge incredulous amusement. Or they had done until she had embarked on this current one and found herself in the same position as the protagonist. . . .

It was called *Foetid Flesh,* a ridiculous title for a start. If you spelt foetid with an O no one could pronounce it and if you left the O out no one would know what it meant. Adultery again, too. Infidelity had been the theme of *Blood Feud* and *Bright Hair about the Bone,* but in those days she hadn't felt the need to identify.

Tonight she was particularly sensitive and she found herself wincing as she reread the typed page. Three literal mistakes in twenty-five lines. . . . She lit a cigarette and wandered into the hall where she gazed at her own reflection in the long glass. Tactless Doris had hit the nail on the head when she said it didn't matter how good-looking a person's husband or wife was. It must be variety and excitement the Julians and the Louises of this world wanted.

She was thinner now but she still had a good figure and she knew she was pretty. Brown eyes and fair hair were an unusual combination and her hair was naturally fair, still the same shade it had been when she was Paul's age. Julian used to say she reminded him of the girl in some picture by Millais.

All that had made no difference. She had done her best to be a good wife but that had made no difference either. Probably Bob was a good husband, a handsome man with a pleasing personality any woman might be proud of. She turned away from the mirror, aware that she was beginning to bracket herself and her next-door neighbour. It made her uneasy and she tried to dismiss him from her mind.

Chapter Two

Susan had just left Paul and Richard at the school gates when Bob North's car passed her. That was usual, a commonplace daily happening. This morning, however, instead of joining the High Street stream that queued to enter the North Circular, the car pulled into the kerb a dozen yards ahead of her and Bob, sticking his head out of the window, went through the unmistakable dumbshow of the driver offering someone a lift.

She went up to the car, feeling a slight trepidation at this sudden show of friendship. 'I was going shopping in Harrow,' she said, certain it would be out of his way. But he smiled easily.

'Fine,' he said. 'As it happens, I have to go into Harrow. I'm leaving the car for a big service. I'll have to go in by train tomorrow, so let's hope the weather cheers up.'

For Susan was glad to embark upon this dreary and perennial topic. She got into the car beside him, remembering an editorial of Julian's in which he had remarked that the English, although partakers in the most variable and quixotic climate in the world, never become used to its vagaries, but comment upon them with shock and resentment as if all their lives had been spent in the predictable monsoon. And despite Julian's scornful admonitions, Susan now took up Bob's cue. Yesterday had been mild, today was damp with an icy wind. Spring was certainly going to be late in coming. He listened to it all, replying in kind, until she felt his embarrassment must be as great as her own. Was he already regretting having said a little too much the night before? Perhaps he had offered her the lift in recompense; perhaps he was anxious not to return to their old footing of casual indifference but attempting to create an easier neighbourly friendship. She must try to keep the conversation on this level. She mustn't mention Louise.

They entered the North Circular where the traffic was heavy and Susan racked her brains for something to say.

'I'm going to buy a present for Paul, one of those electrically operated motorways. It's his birthday on Thursday.'

'Thursday, is it?' he said, and she wondered why, taking his eyes briefly from the busy road, he gave her a quick indecipherable glance. Perhaps she had been as indiscreet in mentioning her son as in talking of Louise. Last night he had spoken of his sorrow at his childlessness. 'Thursday,' he said again, but not interrogatively this time. His hands tightened a little on the wheel and the bones showed white.

'He'll be six.'

She knew he was going to speak then, that the moment had come. His whole body seemed to grow tense beside her and she perceived in him that curious holding of the breath and almost superhuman effort to conquer inhibition that precedes the outpouring of confession or confidence.

The Harrow bus was moving towards its stop and she was on the point of telling him, of saying that she could easily get out here and bus the rest of the way, when he said with an abruptness that didn't fit his words, 'Have you been very lonely?'

That was unexpected, the last question she had been prepared for. 'I'm not sure what you mean,' she said hesitantly.

'I said, have you been lonely? I mean since your divorce.'

'Well, I . . .' Her cheeks burned and she looked down into her lap, at the blackleather gloves that lay limply like empty useless hands. Her own hands clenched, but she relaxed them deliberately. 'I've got over it now,' she said shortly.

'But at the time, immediately afterwards,' he persisted.

The first night had been the worst. Not the first night she and Julian had slept apart but the night after the day when he had gone for good. She had stood at the window for hours, watching the people come and go. It had seemed to her then that no one but herself in the whole of her little world was alone. Everyone had an ally, a partner, a lover. Those married couples she could see had never seemed so affectionate, so bound together, before. Now she could remember quite distinctly how Bob and Louise had come home late from some dance or party, had laughed together in their front garden and gone into the house hand in hand.

She wasn't going to tell him any of that. 'Of course, I had a lot of adjusting to do,' she said, 'but lots of women get deserted by their husbands. I wasn't unique.'

Plainly he had no intention of wasting sympathy on her case. 'And husbands by their wives,' he said. Here we go, Susan thought. Surely it couldn't take more that ten minutes before they got to Harrow? 'We're in the same boat, Susan.'

'Are we?' She didn't raise her eyebrows; she gave him no cue.

'Louise is in love with someone else.' The words sounded cold, deliberate, matter-of-fact. But when Susan made no reply, he suddenly burst out raggedly, 'You're a discreet, cagey one, aren't you? Louise ought to thank you. Or maybe you're on her side. Yes, I suppose that's what it is. You've got a big anti-men thing because of what happened to you. It would be different, wouldn't it, if some girl came calling on me while Louise was out of the house?'

Susan said quietly, although her hands were shaking, 'It was kind of you to give me a lift. I didn't know I was expected to show my gratitude by telling you what your wife does while you're out.'

He caught his breath. 'Perhaps that's what I did expect.'

'I don't want to have any part in your private life, yours and Louise's. Now I'd like to get out, please.'

He reacted peculiarly to this. Susan had thought refusal impossible, but instead of slowing the car down, he swung with hardly any warning into the fast lane. A car immediately behind them braked and hooted. Bob down hard on the accelerator and Susan saw his mouth ease into the smile of triumph. Indignant as she was for a moment she was also genuinely afraid. There was something wild and ungoverned in his face that some women might have found attractive, but to Susan he simply looked very young, a reckless child.

The needle on the speedometer climbed. There were men who thought fast dangerous driving a sign of virility and this perhaps was what he wanted to demonstrate. His pride had been hurt and she mustn't hurt it further. So instead of protesting, she only said dryly, although her palms were wet, 'I should hardly have thought your car was in need of a service.'

He gave a low unhappy chuckle. 'You're a nice girl, Susan. Why didn't I have the sense to marry someone like you?' Then he put out the indicator, slowed and took the turn. 'Did I frighten you? I'm sorry.' He bit his lip. 'I'm so damned unhappy.' He sighed and put his left hand up to his forehead. The dark lock fell across it and once more Susan saw the bewildered boy. 'I suppose he's with her now, leaving his car outside for everyone to see. I can picture it all. That ghastly dog barks and they all go to their windows. Don't they? Don't they, Susan?'

'I suppose so.'

'For two pins I'd drop to lunch one day and catch them.'

'That's the shop I want, Bob, so if you wouldn't mind . . .'

'And that's my garage.'

He got out and opened the door for her courteously. Julian had never bothered with small attentions of this kind. Julian's face had never shown what he was feeling. Bob was far better looking than Julian, franker, easier to know—and yet? It wasn't a kind face, she thought. There was sensitivity there, but of the most egocentric kind, the sensitivity that feels itself, closes itself to the pains of others, demands, grasps, suffers only when its possessor is thwarted.

She stepped out of the car and stood on the pavement beside him in the cold wind. It whipped colour into the skin over his cheekbones so that suddenly he looked healthy and carefree. Two girls went past them and one of them looked back at Bob, appraisingly, calculatingly, in the way men look at pretty women. He too had caught the glance and it was something of a shock to Susan to watch him preen himself faintly and lean against the car with conscious elegance. She picked up her basket and said briskly, 'Thanks. I'll see you around.'

'We must do this more often,' he said with a shade of sarcasm.

The car was still at the pavement edge and he still sitting at the wheel when she came out of the toyshop. How hard the past year had made her! Once she would would have felt deeply for anyone in his situation, her own situation of twelve months before. She couldn't escape the feeling he was acting a part, putting all the energy he could muster into presenting himself as an object of pity. He said he was unhappy, but he didn't look unhappy. He looked as if he wanted people to think he was. Where were the lines of strain, the silent miserable reserve? Their eyes met for a second and she could have sworn he made his mouth droop for her benefit. He raised his hand in a brief salute, started the engine and moved off along the concrete lane between the petrol pumps.

In another *Certainty* editorial, Julian Townsend had averred that almost the only green spaces remaining in north-west London were cemeteries. One of these, the overspill graveyard of some central borough, separated the backgardens of Orchard Drive from the North Circular Road. From a distance it still had a prettiness, an almost rural air, for the elms still raised their black skeletal arms against the sky and rooks still nested in them. But, taking the short cut home across the cemetery, you could only forget you were in a suburb, on the perimeter of a city, by the exercise of great imagination and by half closing your senses. Instead of scented grass and pine needles, you smelt the sourness of the chemical factory, and between the trees the traffic could always be seen as if on an eternal senseless conveyor belt, numberless cars, transporters carrying more cars, scarlet buses.

Susan got off one of those buses and took the cemetery path home. A funeral had taken place the day before and a dozen wreaths lay on the fresh mound, but a night of frost and half a day of bitter wind had curled and blackened their petals. It was still cold. The clouds were amorphous, dishcloth-coloured, with ragged edges where the wind tore them. A day, Susan thought, calculated to depress even the most cheerful. Struggling across the bleakest part of the expanse, she thought that to an observer she must appear as she held her coat collar up against her cheeks like Oliver Twist's mother on her last journey to the foundling hospital. Then she smiled derisively. At least she wasn't pregnant or poor or homeless.

Now as she came into the dip on the Matchdown Park side, she could see the backs of the Orchard Drive houses. Her own and the Norths' were precisely identical and this brought her a feeling of sadness and waste. It seemed too that their occupants' lives were destined to follow a similar pattern, distrust succeeding love, bitterness and rupture, distrust.

Two men were coming down the path from Louise's back door. They had cups of tea in their hands, the steam making faint plumes in the chill air, and Susan supposed they were labourers from the excavations on the road immediately below her. They had been digging up that bit of tarmac for weeks now, laying drains or cables—who knew what they ever did?—but it had never occurred to Susan to offer them tea. To her they had merely meant the nuisance of having clay brought in on Paul's shoes and the staccato screaming chatter of their pneumatic drills.

She let herself out of the cemetery gate and crossed the road. Inside the workmen's hut a red fire burned in a brazier made from a perforated bucket. As she approached the gate in her own fence the heat from this fire reached her, cheerful, heartening, a warm acrid breeze.

The men who had the tea cups moved up to the fire and squatted in front of it. Susan was about to say good morning to them when a third emerged from the trench that never seemed to grow deeper or shallower and gave a shrill wolf whistle. No woman ever really minds being whistled at. Does any woman ever respond? Susan fixed her face into the dead-pan expression she reserved for such occasions and entered her own garden.

Out of the corner of her eye, she saw the whistling man march up Louise's path in quest of his tea. The fence was six feet high between the two back doors. Susan could see nothing, but she heard Louise laugh and the exchange of badinage that followed that laughter.

Susan went through the house and out of the front door to bring in the milk. Contrary to Bob's prediction, there was no green Zephyr on the grass patch, but wedged into the earth at the far side of the garden she caught sight of its counterpart in miniature. Inadvertently she had left one of Paul's cars out all night.

As she stooped to pick it up, shaking the earth from its wheels, Doris appeared from Betty Gibbs's house with Betty following her to prolong their conversation and their last goodbyes as far as the gate.

'An endless stream of them,' Susan heard Betty say, 'always up and down the path. Why can't they make their own tea? They've got a fire. Oh, hallo.' Susan had been spotted. She moved towards them,

wishing she felt less reluctant. 'Doris and I have been
watching the way our neighbour runs her canteen.'

'No visit from lover-boy today,' said Doris. 'That's
what it is.'

'Louise has been making tea for those men for
weeks and weeks,' Susan protested, and as she did so
she felt a violent self-disgust. Who decreed that she
should always find herself in the role of Louise's defend-
ing counsel? The woman was nothing to her, less than
nothing. How smug she must appear to these perfectly
honest, ordinary neighbours! Smug and censorious and
disapproving. There was earth on her hands and now
she found herself brushing it off fastidiously as if it
were a deeper defilement. 'Come,' she said and she
managed an incredulous smile, 'you don't really think
Louise is interested in any of those workmen?'

'I know *you* don't. You're too discreet to live.'

'I'm sorry, Doris. I don't mean to be a prig.' Susan
took a deep breath. 'I just hope things will work out
for the Norths, that's all, and that they won't be too
unhappy.'

The other two women seemed for a moment taken
aback. It was as if unhappiness as the outcome of the
Norths' difficulties had never occurred to them. Excitement, perhaps, or huge scandal or further sensational
food for speculation, but nothing as real as grief. Doris
tossed her head and Susan waited for the sharp retort.
Instead Doris said mildly and too loudly, 'I'll be in
with Paul at the usual time.'

It was a sound characteristic of Louise North that
had altered her and caused the swift artificial change of
subject. Behind them on the Braeside path came the
sharp clatter of the metal-tipped high heels Louise always wore. Roped into this conspiracy of gossip, Susan
didn't turn round. Her back was towards Louise but
the other women faced her and it was both comic and
distasteful to see the way they drew themselves up before Betty, the weaker of the two, managed a feeble
smile and a twitch of the head.

Susan would have felt less weary of them and less

sickened had they accorded the same treatment to Julian a year ago. But as soon as trouble between her husband and herself became evident these women had positively fawned on him. In Matchdown Park, surely the last bastion of Victorianism, the adulterer was still fascinating, the adulteress fallen. Deliberately she crossed back into her own garden and gave Louise a broad smile and a hearty untypical, 'Hallo, there!'

Her neighbour had come into the garden on the same mission as her own and in her hands she held two pint bottles of milk, their foil tops pecked to pieces by blue tits. 'Hallo,' said Louise in her little girl's voice that always had a whine in it.

'Bob gave me a lift into Harrow this morning.'

'Oh, yes?' Louise couldn't have sounded less interested, but just the same she approached the fence, picking her way across the soggy grass. Her heels sank in just as her lover's car tyres had sunk into the grass plot.

Louise always wore very high heels. Without them she would have been less than five feet tall, about the size of a girl of twelve, but like most tiny women she set herself perpetually on stilts and piled her hair into a stack on top of her head. Beneath it her little white face looked wizened and shrunken. Of course, it was particularly cold this morning and as usual Doris had begun to shout about the low temperature at the top of her voice, reiterating her urgent desire to get back to her fire as she made her slow way back across the road.

'Freezing! I've never known such weather. Goodness knows why we don't all pack up and go to Australia!'

'It isn't as cold as all that,' Louise whispered, and now she was leaning over the fence. It only reached to the average persons waist, but she rested her elbows on it and stared wistfully at Susan. 'There are worse things,' she said, 'than a bit of cold.'

'I must want my head tested, hanging about here,' Doris shouted, still on the pavement, still staring frankly at Louise. 'I'm a mass of chilblains as it is.'

'Well, I really am going in,' Susan said firmly and she closed the front door behind her. For a moment she had had the uneasy notion that Louise too wanted to confide in her, only it was impossible. She hardly knew the woman. The idea that an intimacy might be about to grow between her and Norths really frightened her. Yesterday they had been the merest acquaintances, while now ... It almost seemed that Julian had been right when he said you chose your friends but your neighbours were thrust upon you and the only protection was to hold yourself aloof. No doubt, she had been too forthcoming. It might even be that her reputation for discretion at which Doris had hinted had reached the Norths' ears, so that separately they had decided to make use of her as the repository of their secrets.

Susan shrugged, hardened her heart and settled herself at her desk. It was a bore, but there was nothing to be afraid of. And why did she suddenly feel this curious dichotomy, this desire both to be miles away and at the same time to go outside once more and look at Braeside, that strangely secret house where the windows were seldom opened and where no child ever played on the lawn? It was as if she wanted to reassure herself, to settle a doubt or allay a fear.

Presently she spread her hands across the keys and emptied her mind.

At half past three she went into the kitchen. A resolution had been forming subconsciously while she worked and now she brought it out into the open. In future she would have as little as possible to do with the Norths. No more accepting of lifts, no more garden talks. It might even be prudent to be on the alert for their comings and goings to avoid bumping into them.

The drills were screaming behind the back fence. Susan put the kettle on, watching the big elms sway in the wind with the pliability of grass blades. From here she could just see the workmen's fire glowing crimson in its punctured bucket and the workmen's faces, 'dark faces pale against the rosy flame' as they passed across the threshold of their hut. The sight of another's hearth which others share and enjoy always brings a sense of exclusion and of loneliness. The brazier, incandescent and vivid, its flames burning translucent blue against the red heart, brought to mind the improvised stoves of chestnut sellers and she remembered how she and Julian, on their way to a theatre, had sometimes stopped to buy and warm their hands.

The sky was blue now like arctic ice and the clouds which tumbled across it were pillowy glacial floes. Susan's kettle bumped, the drills shrilled and then, clearly and succinctly through the louder sounds, there came a gentle tap at the front door.

Pollux hadn't barked. It must be a neighbour or a familiar visitor to the street. Surely it was too early for Doris to be bringing Paul? Besides, Doris always came to the back door and Doris always shouted and banged.

The drills died away on a whine. Susan crossed the hall and the little tap was repeated. She opened the door and when she saw who her caller was she felt an actual dismal sinking of the heart.

What was the use of resolving to avoid people when those people intruded themselves upon you? Louise North wasn't wearing her little girl's size eight coat, but had wrapped it round her thin shoulders. She stepped inside, shivering, before Susan could hinder her and the little hammer heels rattled on the wood-block floor. Louise was trembling, she was scarcely steady on her feet.

'Spare me five minutes, Susan? Five minutes to talk?' She lifted her eyes, bending her head back to look up into Susan's face. Those eyes, the pale insipid blue of glass beads, were watering from the cold. But she's only come from next door, Susan thought, unless she's crying. She *is* crying. 'You don't mind if I call you Susan, do you? You must call me Louise.'

You're at the end of your tether. Susan almost said it aloud. Two tears coursed down Louise's thin face.

She brushed at them and scuttled towards the living-room. 'I know the way' she muttered. 'It's just the same as my house.' Her heels left a twin trail of little pits, ineradicable permanent holes in the parquet.

Susan followed her helplessly. Louise's face was muddy with make-up applied over stale make-up and tear-stains. Now in the warm quiet living-room she dropped her head into her hands and tears trickled through her fingers on to the gooseflesh of her wrists.

Chapter Three

Susan stood by the window and waited for Louise to stop crying. She was anxious not to prejudice her, but she felt impatient. Louise had no handkerchief. Now, in a feeble and embarrassed way, she was fumbling in the pockets of her coat and looking vaguely about her for the handbag she hadn't brought.

In the kitchen the kettle was bumping on the gas. Susan knew it was the sponge she had put inside it years and years ago to absorb the lime deposit the water made. The sponge had become petrified with time and the noise of this piece of rock lurching against the kettle lining made the only sound. Susan went into the kitchen, turning off the gas and fetched Louise a clean handkerchief.

'I'm ever so sorry,' Louise gulped. The tears had made her childish face pink and puffy. She put up a hand to her hair, retrieving wisps and poking them back into the piled lacquered structure that gave her an extra two inches. 'You must think me very uncontrolled, coming here and breaking down like this when we hardly know each other.' She bit her lip and went on miserably. 'But my friends are all Catholics, you see, and I don't like to talk to them about it. I mean, Father O'Hara and Eileen and people like that. I know what they'd say.'

Susan had forgotten Louise was a Catholic. Now she remembered seeing her go off to church sometimes with Eileen O'Donnell, black lace scarves in their hands to put over their heads at the mass. 'Of course, I can't get a divorce,' Louise said, 'but I thought—Oh, dear, I can't put it into words. I've taken up your time getting into a state and now I can't seem to say it.' She gave Susan a sidelong glance. 'I'm like you, you see, I'm rather reserved.'

Susan didn't altogether care for the comparison. Reserve doesn't take itself into a neighbour's house and weep and borrow handkerchiefs. 'Well, suppose you sit there and calm down a bit while I make the tea?'

'You're awfully kind, Susan.'

The drills began their deafening clamour while Susan was cutting bread and butter. She began to think what she should say to Louise when she returned to the living-room, but she feared any advice she could give would differ hardly at all from that proffered by Eileen or the priest. As to what Louise was about to say to her, she had no difficulty at all in guessing. It would be a defiant recital of how love gave you the right to do as you chose; how it was better to spoil one life now than ruin two for ever; how you must take what you can get while you were still young. Julian had said it all already and had expressed it more articulately than Louise ever would. Should there be any hesitations or gaps in her narrative, Susan thought bitterly, she could always provide excuses from Julian's own logical and entirely heartless apologia. She went back with the teacloth and the plates. Louise was standing up now, watching the quivering elms and the cold rushing sky, her face stricken with woe.

'Feeling a bit better?' Susan asked, and she added rather repressively, 'Paul will be in in a moment.' She hoped her face made it plain to her visitor that she didn't want her son, the child of a broken marriage and already the witness of grown-up grief, to hear yet again an adult's marital problems and see an adult's tears.

But Louise, like her husband, had little interest or

concern to spare for other people's anxieties. 'Oh, dear,' she said pathetically, 'and Doris Winter with him, I suppose. Susan, I've been screwing up my courage all afternoon to come to you. It took me hours and hours before I dared. But you were so nice and friendly to me in the garden and I . . . Look, Bob's going to be late tonight and I'll be all alone. Would you come in to me? Just for an hour?'

The side gate clicked and slammed. For a second the two women's eyes met and Susan thought how innocent Louise looked. As if she wouldn't hurt a fly. Why bother with flies when you can torture people?

'Hi, there!' Doris called from the back door. 'Late again. I'm dying for a cup of tea.'

'Will you stay and have one?'

Louise shook her head and picked up her coat from the chair. Her face was still blotched and tear-stained. She looked up when Doris came in and a small pathetic smile trembled on her lips.

'Oh, I didn't know you'd got company,' said Doris, 'or I wouldn't have come bursting in.' Her eyes were wide with excitement at the idea she might by chance have come upon adventure at the least likely time and in the least likely place. She drew her stiff red fingers out of the woollen gloves and, turning towards Susan, raised an interrogatory eyebrow. Susan didn't respond and it amused her to see Doris's greedy anticipation gradually give way to chagrin until, like a battery in need of recharging from some source of power, she attached herself to the radiator and said sulkily, 'All right for some. I've been frozen all day.'

Then Louise said it. Afterwards Susan often thought that if her neighbour had kept silent or merely made some harmless rejoinder, the whole ensuing tragedy would have taken a different course or perhaps have been altogether averted. In spite of her determination not to be involved, she would have accepted Louise's invitation for that night out of weakness and pity. She would have learned and understood and been in a position to defend.

But Louise, fumbling with her coat and hesitating whether to pocket Susan's handkerchief or leave it on the chair arm, turned those watery glass bead eyes on Doris and said, 'I'll have my central heating next winter. They're soon going to put it in.' A tiny spark of enthusiasm brought colour into her cheeks. 'I expect you've seen the man here.'

Doris's always active eyebrows jerked as if she had a tic and almost disappeared into her fringe.

'I'll just see you to the door,' Susan said coldly. Rage bit off the christian name she had meant to use and which would have softened the dismissal. That Louise should come here and cry about her love affair, then persist in employing the blind she had used to deceive everyone, filled her with choking anger. The dishonesty and the duplicity were past bearing.

Louise tripped as she crossed the hall and Susan didn't put out a hand to steady her. The metal heel left a pit and a long gash in the parquet Susan and her cleaner, Mrs. Dring, kept so carefully polished. Illogically, this wanton damage was more maddening than Louise's slyness and her lack of control. At the front door she stopped and whispered:

'You'll come tonight?'

'I'm afraid I can't leave Paul.'

'Come tomorrow then, for coffee,' Louise pleaded. 'Come as soon as you've taken Paul to school.'

Susan sighed. It was on the tip of her tongue to say she would never come, that the Norths and their problems were nothing to her. Bob would be away for once, so like a child, Louise wanted Susan's shoulder to cry on. Didn't it occur to her that Susan was always alone, that Julian had gone away for good? It was all Julian's fault. If he had been here, he wouldn't have allowed her to be the Norths' mediator and counsellor, but then if he had been here none of this confiding would have begun. It was only because she had been deserted and divorced that the Norths thought her a suitable adviser. Her experiences qualified her; she might be supposed to understand the motives of wife and husband; her knowledge gave her the edge over the priest and the devout unworldly friends.

'Louise . . .' she said helplessly, opening the door and letting the chill damp air wash over her hot face.

'Please, Susan. I know it's ugly and beastly, but I can't help it. Please say you'll come.'

'I'll come at eleven,' Susan said. She could no longer resist that look of agonised supplication. Still exasperated but almost resigned, she followed Louise outside to call the boys in for their tea.

Louise's heels tap-tapped away into the side entrance. Her shoes had pointed toes, curled and wrinkled at the tips where her own toes were too short to reach. In her long floppy coat and those absurd over-large shoes, she reminded Susan of a little girl dressing up in her mother's clothes.

For a moment Susan let her gaze travel over the Braeside façade. Of all the houses in the street it was the only one whose occupants had never troubled to improve its appearance. Susan was no admirer of rustic gnomes, of carriage lamps or birdbaths on Doric pediments, but she recognised a desire for individuality in the Gibbs's potted bay tree, a wistful need of beauty in the O'Donnells' window boxes.

Braeside was as stark now as it must have been when it was first built ten years before. Since that time it had never been painted and the perpetually closed windows looked as if they would never open. The house belonged to the Norths and yet it had an air of property rented on a short lease as if its owners regarded it as a place of temporary sojourn rather than a home.

No trees had been planted in the front garden. Almost every other house had a kanzan or cypresses or a prunus. The Braeside garden was just a big square of earth planted entirely with daffodils and with a few inches of turf bordering it. The daffodils looked as if they were grown by a market gardener to sell, they stood in such straight rows. But Louise never even cut them. Susan could remember how in springs gone by she had sometimes seen her neighbour walk carefully between the rows to touch the waxen green leaves or stoop to smell the fresh and faintly acrid scent of their blossoms.

They were as yet only in bud, each tightly folded yellow head as sealed as the house itself and like it, seeming to hold secrets.

Susan called the children and hustled them in through the side gate. The Braeside windows looked black and opaque, effective shutters for a woman to hide behind and cry her eyes out.

Coping repressively with Doris's curiosity and trying to give Paul an adequate but necessarily untruthful answer to his question as to why Mrs North had been crying, left Susan exhausted and cross. She badly needed someone with whom she could discuss this crisis in the Norths' lives and she thought rather wistfully of how Doris might be now regaling John with its latest phase. A man would see the whole matter more straightforwardly—and less subtly—than she could; a man would advise how to avoid involvement with kindness and tact.

When the phone rang at seven-thirty she knew it must be Julian and for a moment she thought seriously of casting her troubles on his shoulders. If only Julian were more human, less the counterpart of an actor playing a brittle role in an eternal drawing-room comedy! And since his new marriage he had grown even more suave and witty and in a way unreal. Contemptuous he had always been, misanthropic and exclusive, besides having this odd conviction of his that dwellers in a suburb were quite alien to himself, subhuman creatures leading a vegetable or troglodyte existence. He was indifferent to their activities, although the doings of his own circle often aroused in him an almost feminine curiosity, and as soon as Susan heard his voice her hopes went. Consulting Julian would be only to invite a scathing rebuff.

'You said this was the most convenient time,' said

the drawling pendantic voice, 'so, since I aim to please, I've dragged myself away in the middle of my prawn cocktail.'

'Hallo, Julian.'

His habit of plunging into the middle of things without greeting, preamble or announcing who he was, always irritated her. Of course an ex-wife might be expected to recognise her ex-husband's voice; that was fair enough. But Susan knew he did it to everyone, to the remotest acquaintance. In his own estimation he was unique, and it was unthinkable to him that even the deaf or the phone-shy could mistake him for anyone else.

'How are you?'

'I am well.' This strictly correct but unidiomatic reply was another Julianism. He was never 'fine' or even 'very well'. 'How are things in Matchdown Park?'

'Much the same,' said Susan, bracing herself for the sneer.

'I was afraid of that. Now, listen, my dear, I'm afraid Sunday's out as far as having Paul is concerned. Elizabeth's mamma wants us for the weekend and naturally I can't chicken out of that even if I want to, which I don't.'

'I suppose you could take him with you.'

'Lady Maskell isn't exactly mad about having tots around the place.'

It had always seemed odd to Susan that Julian, the editor of a left-wing review, should in the first place have married a baronet's daughter and secondly should set so much store by the landed gentry to which his in-laws belonged.

'This is the second time since Christmas you've put him off,' she said. 'It seems rather pointless the judge making an order for you to have him every fourth Sunday if you're always going to be too busy. He was looking forward to it.'

'Oh, you can take him out somewhere. Take him to the zoo.'

'It's his birthday the day after tomorrow. I thought I'd better remind you.'

'Flap not, my dear. Elizabeth's got it down on her shopping list to make sure we keep it in mind.'

'That's fine then, isn't it?' Susan's voice shook with annoyance. It had been an impossible day, thronged with impossible people. 'You'd better get back to your steak,' she said in the nagging tone he both provoked and hated, 'or whatever's next on the menu.' Elizabeth had got it on her shopping list! Susan could imagine that list: canned prawns, peppers, cocktail sticks, birthday present for 'tot', fillet steak, chocs for Mummy. . . . How maddening Julian was! Strange that whereas remembered words and phrases of his could sadden her and awaken pain, these weekly telephone conversations never did.

He was bound to send Paul something utterly ridiculous, an electric guitar or a skin-diving outfit, neither of which were outside the bounds of what Julian or Elizabeth would consider suitable for a middle-class suburban child on his sixth birthday. Susan went around the house bolting the doors for the night. Usually on this evening task she never bothered to glance up at the side of Braeside, but tonight she did and it disquieted her to see the place in darkness.

Could Louise already have gone to bed? It was scarcely eight o'clock. A simple curiosity, an inquisitiveness as indefensible as Doris's possessed her, drawing her into the front garden to stare frankly at the house next door. It was a blot of darkness amid its brightly lit neighbours. Perhaps Louise had gone out. Very likely she had gone out to meet her lover and was now sitting with him in some characterless North Circular Road pub or holding hands in a half-empty cafe. But Susan didn't think she had and it depressed her to imagine Louise lying sleepless in that house with her eyes open on the dark.

She listened, hardly knowing what she was listening for. She heard nothing and then, a little unnerved, she listened to the silence. Julian called Matchdown Park a dormitory and at night it was a dormitory indeed, its denizens enclosed like bees in their warm cells. And yet it was incredible that so many people should live and breathe around her, all in utter silence.

But if this was silence, it was nothing to the deep mute soundlessness of the back garden. Susan checked her back door lock, noticing that the wind had died. There was no movement in the black trees and, apart from the running river of traffic in the distance, no light but from the three red spots of the lamps the workmen had left on their pyramid of clay.

Chapter Four

David Chadwick hadn't seen Bernard Heller for months and then, quite by chance, he bumped into him on a Tuesday evening in Berkeley Square. It was outside Stewart and Ardern's and Heller had his arms full of cardboard boxes. Some heating equipment, David thought, that he must be going to dump at the offices in Hay Hill where *Equatair* had its headquarters.

Heller didn't look particularly pleased to see him, although he forced his features into an unsuccessful grin. David, on the other hand, was glad they had met. Last summer, on a generous impulse, he had lent Heller his slide projector and now he thought it was time he got it back.

'How are things?'

'Oh, so-so.' The boxes were stacked up under Heller's chin and perhaps it was this which gave to his face a set look.

'How about a drink if you're knocking off?'

'I've got some more stuff to unload.'

'I'll give you a hand,' David said firmly. He didn't want to lose him now.

'In the car, then.'

He still had the same green Zephyr Six, David noted

as he lifted out the three remaining boxes from the boot which Heller had opened. The cardboard was torn on the top one and inside part of a gas burner could be seen.

'Thanks,' Heller said, and then, with an effort to be gracious, 'Thanks very much, David.'

Equatair's swing doors were still open. A couple of typists in white boots and fun furs passed them on the steps. Heller put his boxes on the floor of a small vestibule and David followed suit. Photographs of radiators and boilers and one of a lush living-room interior were pinned to the walls. It reminded David of his own designs for television film sets. That was how he had first met Heller, through work. *Equatair* made fireplaces too and David had borrowed one for the set of a series called, *Make Mine Crime*.

'How about that drink?'

'All right. I'm in no hurry to get home.' Heller didn't look at David when he said this and he mumbled something else with his head averted. It might have been, 'God knows, I'm not,' but David couldn't be sure of that.

He was a big heavy man, this heating engineer, with a round bullet head and hair that stuck up in short curly bristles. Usually he was almost irritatingly cheerful, inclined to slap people on the back while he told tedious jokes which, for all that had about them an innocent slapstick quality. Tonight he had a hangdog look and David thought he had lost weight. His plump jowls sagged and they were greyish, perhaps not just because Heller, normally careful of his appearance, was in need of shave.

'There's a nice little place in Berwick Street I sometimes go to,' David said. He hadn't got his car with him so they went in Heller's. For an engineer-cum-salesman, he was a lousy driver, David thought. Twice he was afraid they were going to go into the back of a taxi. It was his first experience of being driven by Heller as their encounters had usually been for a pre-lunch drink or a sandwich. Heller had been kindness itself over the fireplace and almost embarrassingly generous. It had been a job to stop him paying for all their drinks. Then, back in July, he had happened to say his twin brother had been staying with relatives in Switzerland—they were Swiss or half-Swiss or something—but couldn't show the slides he had taken because he hadn't a projector. For a long time David had wanted to show his gratitude, but it was difficult while Heller insisted on paying for everything. The loan of the projector had settled that question.

Paying off debts was one thing. He hadn't expected the man to hang on to it for eight months without a word.

'I wonder if I might have my projector back sometime?' he said as they crossed Regent Street. 'The summer's coming and holidays . . .'

'Oh, sure,' Heller said without enthusiasm. 'I'll drop it off at the studios, shall I?'

'Please.' It wouldn't have hurt him to say thank you. Still, he evidently had something on his mind. 'That's the place, The Man in the Iron Mask. If you're quick you can nip in between that van and the Mercedes.'

Heller wasn't very quick. Twice he bungled the reversing manoeuvre. The pub was tucked between an Indonesian restaurant and a strip club. Heller gave the pictures of nudes on leopard skin a sick look.

Over the entrance to The Man in the Iron Mask was a sign depicting his apocryphal character, his head encased in a cage. David went in first. Inside the place was cosy and overheated and with its black and white tiled floor and walls panelled in dark wood, suggested a Dutch interior. But the hunting prints could only be English and nowhere but in England would you see the facetious slogans and the pinned-up cartoons.

The area behind the bar was suffused with red light, making it look like the entrance to a furnace, and this same light stained the faces of the man and the girl who sat there. Her fingernails showed mauve when she moved her hands out of the red glow to caress her boy-friend's shoulders. The discerning would have recognised his grey tunic as the upper half of a Confederate uniform.

'What are you going to have?' David asked, anticipating the usual. 'No, let me.'

'Lime and lager,' Heller said only.

'Big stuff. What are we celebrating?'

'It's just that I have to drive.'

David went up to the bar. He was trying to remember where Heller lived. South London somewhere. If he was going to have to make conversation with this semi-conscious man, he would need something strong.

'Double scotch and a lime and lager, please,' he said to the barman.

'You mean lager and lime.'

'I don't suppose it would matter at that.'

Heller rubbed his big forehead as if it ached. 'D'you often come in here?'

'Off and on. It's quiet. You see some interesting characters.' And as he spoke, the Confederate kissed his girl on her oyster-coloured mouth. The door opened with an abrupt jerk and two bearded men came in.

They advanced to the bar and, because it was for an instant unattended, knocked sharply on the counter. The taller of the two, having given their order with a scowl, resumed an anecdote. The red glow turned his beard to ginger.

'So I said to this bank manager chappie, "It's all very well you moaning about my overdraft," I said. "Where would your lot be without overdrafts?" I said, "That's what I'd like to know. That's what keeps you banks going. You'd be out of a job, laddie," I said.'

'Quite,' said the other man.

Heller didn't even smile. His florid skin was puckered about his eyes and the corners of his mouth turned down.

'How's work?' David asked desperately.

'Just the same.'

'Still operating in the Wembley-Matchdown Park area?'

Heller nodded and mumbled into his glass, 'Not for long.'

David raised an eyebrow.

'I'm going abroad. Switzerland.'

'Then we are celebrating. I seem to remember your once saying that's what you wanted. Haven't *Equatair* got a footing out there?'

'Zurich.'

'When do you go?'

'May.'

The man's manner was only just short of rude. If he went on like that it was a wonder he ever sold anyone a thermostat replacement, let alone a whole central heating system. It struck David suddenly that May was only two months off. If he ever wanted to see his projector again he had better look sharp about it.

'You're fluent in German, aren't you? Bi-lingual?'

'I went to school in Switzerland.'

'You must be excited.' It was a stupid thing to say, like asking a shivering man if he was hot.

'Oh, I don't know,' Heller said. 'Might have been once.' He finished his drink and a spark of something fierce flashed momentarily in his dark eyes. 'People change, you get older.' He got up. 'There doesn't seem much point in anything, does there?' Without offering to buy David a drink, he said. 'Can I drop you anywhere? Northern Line for you, isn't it?'

David lived alone in a bachelor flat. He wasn't going anywhere that night and he intended to eat out. 'Look, I don't want to be a bore about this,' he said awkwardly, 'but if you're going straight home, would you mind if I came along with you and collected my projector?'

'Now, d'you mean?'

'Well, yes. You're going in May and I dare say you've got a lot on your mind.'

'All right,' Heller said ungraciously. They got into the car and David's spirits improved slightly when the other man said, with a ghost of his old grin, 'Bear with me, old man. I'm not very good company these days. It was decent of you to lend us the projector. I didn't intend to hold on to it.'

'I know that,' David said, feeling much better.

They went over one of the bridges and down past the Elephant and Castle. Heller drove by a twisty route through back streets and although he seemed to know his way, he was careless about traffic lights and once he went over a pedestrian crossing with people on it.

Silence had fallen between them and Heller broke it only to say, 'Nearly there.' The street was full of buses going to places David knew only by name, Kennington, Brixton, Stockwell. On the left-hand side a great blank wall with small windows in it ran for about two hundred yards. It might have been a barracks or a prison. There wasn't a tree or a patch of grass in sight. At a big brightly lit Odeon Heller turned right and David saw that they were at a typical South London crossroads, dominated by a colonnaded church in the Wren style, only Wren had been dead a hundred and fifty years when it was put up. Opposite it was a tube station. David didn't know which one. All he could see was London Transport's Saturn-shaped sign, glowing blue and red. People streamed out over the crossing, their faces a sickly green in the mercury vapour light.

Some of them took a short cut home through a treeless park with a cricket pavilion and public lavatories. Heller drove jumpily on the inside lane of the stream. The street was neither truly shopping centre nor residential. Most of the big old houses were in the process of being pulled down. Shops there were, but all of the same kind, thrust shabbily together in a seemingly endless rhythmic order: off-licence, café, pet foods, betting shop, off-license, café . . . If he were Heller he wouldn't have been able to wait for May. The prospect of Zürich would be like heaven. What kind of a slum did the man live in, anyway?

Not a slum at all. A fairly decent, perhaps ten-year-old block of flats. They were arranged in four storeys around a glass and concrete court. Hengist House. David looked around for Horsa and saw it fifty yards ahead. Some builder with Anglo-Saxon attitudes, he thought, amused.

Heller put the car into a bay marked with white lines.

'We're on the ground floor,' he said. 'Number three.'

The entrance hall looked a bit knocked about. Someone had written, 'Get back to Kingston' on a wall between two green doors. David didn't think they had meant Kingston, Surrey. Heller put his key into the lock of number three. They had arrived.

A narrow passage ran throught the flat to an open bathroom door. Heller didn't call out and when his wife appeared he didn't kiss her.

Seeing her gave David a jolt. Heller was only in his early thirties but he was already touched by the heavy hand of middle-age. This girl looked very young. He hadn't been thinking about her so he had no pre-conceived idea as to how she would look. Nevertheless, he was startled by what he saw and as he met her eyes he knew she expected him to be startled and was pleased.

She wore blue jeans and one of those skinny sweaters that there is no point in wearing if you really are skinny. Her figure was the kind that is photo-graphed large and temptingly in the non-quality Sundays. Long black hair that a brush touch would set sparking fell to her shoulders.

'I don't think you've met,' Heller mumbled, and that was all the introduction David got. Mrs Heller peeled herself from the wall and now her glance was indifferent. 'Make yourself at home. I won't be a minute find-ing the projector.' He looked at his wife. 'That slide projector,' he said. 'Where did you put it when Carl brought it back?'

'In the bedroom cupboard, I suppose.'

Heller showed him into the living-room, if pushing open a door and muttering could be called showing anyone anywhere. Then he went away. The room had three white walls and one red one with a stringed in-strument hanging above *Equatair* radiator. A little bit of haircord clung to the centre of the floor space. Mrs Heller came in and rather ostentatiously placed cutlery for two persons on the table. It amused David to reflect on the domestic surroundings of real salesmen-executives. In the films and plays he did sets for they had open-plan apartments, forty feet long, split level with wall-to-wall carpeting, room dividers festooned with ivy, leather furniture. He sat down in an armchair that was a woven plastic cone in a metal frame. Outside the buses moved in a white and yellow glare.

'Sorry to come bursting in on you like this,' he said. She put two glasses of water on the table. In his films they had bottles of Romani Conti served in straw baskets. 'I happened to run into Bernard and I remembered my projector.'

She swivelled, tilting her chin. 'Ran into him, did you?' Her voice had the remnants of a burr he couldn't place. 'D'you mind telling me where?'

'In Berkeley Square,' he said, surprised.

'Sure it wasn't Matchdown Park?'

'Quite sure.' What was all this? The man was legitimately employed in Matchdown Park, wasn't he? He watched her as she finished laying the table. An orchidaceous face, he thought. Horrible word, but it just described that lush velvety skin, the little nose and the full pink pearl lips. Her eyes were green with gold sparks. 'I hear you're going to Switzerland. Looking forward to it?'

She shrugged. 'Nothing's settled yet.'

'But surely Bernard said . . .'

'You don't want to listen to everything he says.'

David followed her into the kitchen because he couldn't hang about there any longer with the glasses of water and the mandoline or whatever it was. The blue jeans were provocative as she bent to light her cigarette from the gas. He wondered how old she was. Not more than twenty-four or twenty-five. In the next room he could hear Heller banging about, apparently shifting things from a high shelf.

A pan of water was heating on the cooker. Already

cooked and lying dispiritedly on a plate were two small overdone chops. When the water in the pan boiled the girl took it from the gas and emptied into it the contents of a packet labelled, 'Countryman's Supper. Heavenly mashed potatoes in thirty seconds.' David wasn't sorry they weren't going to ask him to share it.

'Magdalene!'

Heller's voice sounded wary and fed-up. So that was her name, Magdalene. She looked up truculently as her husband lumbered in.

'I can't think where it's got to,' Heller said worriedly, glancing with embarrassment at his dusty hands.

'Leave it,' David said. 'I'm keeping you from your meal.'

'Maybe it's up there.' It was the girl who had spoken, indicating a closed cupboard on top of the dresser. David was a little surprised, for up till now, she had shown no interest in the recovery of his property and seemed indifferent as to whether he went or stayed.

Heller dragged out a stool from under the table and stuck it against the dresser on which was a pile of un-ironed linen. His wife watched him open the cupboard and fumble about inside.

'There was a phone call for you,' she said abruptly, her full mouth pouting. 'That North woman.' Heller mumbled something. 'I thought it was a bloody nerve, phoning here.' This time her husband made no reply. 'Damned cheek!' she said, as if trying to provoke from him a spark of anger.

'I hope you didn't forget your manners on the phone.'

David was rather shocked. Uncouth, graceless, Magdalene might be, jealous even. She had hardly deserved to be reproved with such paternal gruffness in front of a stranger. She was evidently drawing breath for an appropriate rejoinder, but David never found out what it would have been. Heller, whose arms and shoulders had been inside the cupboard, retreated and, as he emerged, something heavy and metallic fell out on to the linen.

It was a gun.

David knew next to nothing about firearms. A Biretta or a Mauser, they were all the same to him. He knew only that it was some sort of automatic. It lay there glistening, half on Heller's underpants and half on a pink pillow slip.

Neither of the Hellers said anything. To break the rather ghastly silence, David said facetiously, 'Your secret arsenal?'

Heller started gabbing very fast then. 'I know I shouldn't have it, it's illegal. As a matter of fact, I smuggled it in from the States. Went on a business trip. The Customs don't always look, you know. Magdalene had got scared, being here alone. You get some very funny people about out there, fights, brawls, that kind of thing. Only last week there was a bloke down in the alley shouting at some woman to give him his money. A ponce, I dare say. Hitting her and shouting he was. In Greek,' he added, as if this made things worse.

'It's no business of mine,' David said.

'I just thought you might think it funny.'

Suddenly Magdalene stamped her foot. 'Hurry up, for God's sake. We're going to the pictures at seven-thirty and it's ten past now. And there's the washing-up to do first.'

'I'll do that.'

'Aren't you coming, then?'

'No, thanks.'

She turned off the oven, lifted the plates and carried them into the living-room. David thought she would return, but she didn't. The door closed and faintly from behind it he heard the sound of spy thriller music.

'Here it is at last,' Heller said. 'It was right at the back behind the hair dryer.'

'I've put you to a lot of trouble.'

Heller passed the projector down to him. 'That's one thing I won't have to worry about, anyway,' he said. He didn't close the cupboard doors and he left the gun where it lay.

Perhaps it was the presence of the gun, grim, ugly, vaguely threatening, in this grim and ugly household that made David say on an impulse, 'Look, Bernard, if there's anything I can do . . .'

Heller said stonily, 'Nobody can do anything. Not a magician, are you? Not God? You can't put the clock back.'

'You'll be better when you get to Zürich.'

'If I get there.'

The whole thing had shaken David considerably. Once out of the courtyard, he found himself a pub, bigger and brassier and colder than the Man in the Iron Mask. He had another whisky and then he walked up to the tube station, discovering when he was a few yards from it that it was called East Mulvihill. As he walked under the stone canopy of the station entrance he caught sight of Magdalene Heller on the other side of the street, walking briskly, almost running, towards the big cinema he and Heller had passed. She looked jerkily to right and left before she went in. He watched her unzip her heavy shoulder bag, buy a ticket and go alone up the stairs to the balcony.

The cause of Heller's misery was no longer in doubt. His marriage had gone wrong. One of these ill-assorted, very obviously incompatible people, had transgressed, and from what Magdalene had hinted of a telephone call, David gathered the transgressor was Heller. It looked as if he had found himself another woman. Had he dwindled to this taciturn shadow of the cheerful buffoon he once had been because it was not she but Magdalene he must take with him to Switzerland?

Chapter Five

On the way to school they passed the postman and Paul said, 'I don't have to go to school tomorrow until after he's been, do I?'

'We'll see,' Susan said.

'Well, I shan't,' he said mutinously for Richard's benefit. Richard ran ahead, jumping into the air at intervals to grab at the cherry branches. 'He'll be early anyway,' Paul said in a more conciliatory tone, taking his mother's hand. 'Daddy's going to send me a watch. He promised.'

'A watch! Oh, Paul . . .' Of all the vulnerable and ultimately—when Paul fell over in the playground as he did two or three times a week—tear-provoking presents for a six-year-old! 'You'll have to keep it for best.'

They reached the school gates and the two little boys were absorbed by the throng. Susan looked at the children with different eyes this morning, seeing them as potential adults, makers of misery. A cold melancholy stole over her. Determinedly she braced herself, waved to Paul and turned back towards Orchard Drive.

It was ten to nine, the time she usually saw Bob North. His car regularly passed the school gates about now. Susan didn't want to see him. She remembered their last encounter with distaste. He wouldn't offer her a lift today as he would be able to see she intended to go straight home, but she was certain he would stop. Probably he had found out about Louise's visit to her and their appointment for this morning and he would be anxious to put his own story across before Louise could blacken his character. People in Louise's situation always blamed their marriage partners. Julian had spent a long time pointing out her deficiencies as a wife, her nagging, her dislike of his more *avant-garde* friends, her old-fashioned morality, before embarking on the tale of his own infidelity.

She felt very exposed as she walked back under the cherry trees, nervously aware that any time now Bob's car would nose or back out of the Braeside drive. She thought wildly of bending down to retie her shoelace or, if this ploy failed, diving into the house of someone she slightly knew. The trouble was she hardly knew anyone well enough for that.

It was a still day, not quite foggy, but uniformly grey. Rain threatened in the clammy air. Susan quickened her pace as she approached Braeside and then she remembered. Bob's car was in for a service. He would go to work by train today, so therefore he had probably left much earlier, had certainly left by now. Her spirits lifted absurdly. Really, it was stupid to work herself up to such a nervous pitch because in a couple of hours' time one of her neighbours was going to confide something rather unorthodox to her. That was all it amounted to.

Braeside had a dull dead look. The upstairs curtains were all drawn as if the Norths were away. Perhaps Louise was lying late in bed. Unhappiness made you want to do that. Jane Willingale would have attributed it to a desire to get back to the womb but Susan thought it was only because you felt there was nothing to get up for.

As usual there was not a single open window, not even a fanlight lifted an inch or two. It must be cold and stuffy in there, the air stale with angrily exhaled breath and tears and quarrels.

Mrs Dring would arrive at any moment. Susan let herself into her own warm house and began to grease tins and beat mixture for Paul's party cakes. Her hall clock chimed nine and as the last stroke died away, the pneumatic drills began.

Breaking across this shrill sound, the Airedale's bark sounded hollow. He was used to Mrs Dring by now and wouldn't bark at her arrival. Not for the first time Susan wondered why this canine summons was impossible to resist. Hardly anyone really interesting ever came to Orchard Drive and yet Pollux never barked in vain. She was as vulnerable to the alert as any of the women, although, unlike them, a change of delivery man or a new meter reader left her indifferent. She didn't want to speculate as to why Fortnum's van had called at Gibbs's or a couple of nuns at O'Donnells'. Sometimes she thought she rushed to the window when Pollux barked because, against all experience to the contrary, she always hoped the roar announced a new-comer into her own life, someone who would change it, who would bring hope and joy.

How pathetic and childish, she thought as, in spite of herself, she ran into the living-room and drew aside the curtain. Winters' gate clanged between its concrete posts and Pollux, who had half-mounted it in his rage, dropped back on to the path with a thump.

Susan stared. On the grass patch in the pavement, its tyres buried in the ruts they had made on Monday, stood the green Ford Zephyr.

Once again Louise North was entertaining her lover.

'Good morning, dear. Did you think I wasn't coming?'

Mrs Dring always bellowed this question on a tri-umphant note if she was more than a minute late. A large raw-boned redhead of forty-five, she put immense value on herself and the work she did, confident that her employers, in the event of her non-appearance, must be reduced to a helpless and desperate panic like abandoned infants.

'I'll do downstairs, shall I?' she said, putting her head round the door. 'Make it nice for the boy's party.' Cleaning a room before a children's party seemed pointless to Susan, but it was useless arguing with Mrs Dring. 'Want me to come and give you a hand tomorrow? There's nothing anyone can tell me about running kids' parties. Famous for them I am.'

Mrs Dring didn't explain how she came to know so much about the organisation of children's parties. She had no children of her own. But she was always mak-ing statements of this kind in a dark tone, as if imply-ing that all her acquaintances were aware of her om-nipotent versatility and took repeated advantage of it. She had a good word for no one except her husband, a man whose competence in the most unlikely fields ri-valled her own and who possessed in equal measure to his manual and administrative skills a superhuman in-telligence quotient.

'There's nothing that man doesn't know,' she would say.

Now she advanced into the room and went straight up to the window where she stood tying up her hair, almost scarlet this morning, in a scarf.

'I've been meaning to ask you,' she said, her eye on the green car, 'what's going on next door?'

'Going on?'

'You know what I mean. I got it from my friend who helps Mrs Gibbs. Mind you, my friend's a proper little liar and I reckon anyone who'd believe a word Mrs Gibbs says must want her head tested.' Drawing breath, Mrs Dring proceeded at once to place herself in this lunatic category. 'She says Mrs North is carrying on with the central heating fellow.'

'Do you know him?' Susan couldn't stop herself asking.

'I've seen him about. My husband could tell you his name. You know what a wonderful memory he's got. We was thinking about central heating ourselves and I said, "You want to talk to that fellow—Heffer or Heller or something—who's always about in a green car." But my husband put the pipes in himself in the end. There's nothing he can't do if he puts his mind to it.'

'Why shouldn't he be calling on Mrs North just for business?'

'Yes, funny business. Well, it stands to reason he's in the right job for that kind of thing if he fancies it. It's her I'm disgusted with.' Seeing Susan wasn't to be drawn, Mrs Dring dropped the curtain and pulled two kiss-curls, as fluorescent red as Day-glo paint, out on to her forehead. 'What d'you think of my hair? It's called flamingo, this shade. My husband did it last night. I always tell him he ought to have gone into the trade. He'd have been in the West End by now.'

Susan began typing desultorily. Mrs Dring was never silent for long and these mornings she was on edge, constantly distracted from work by futile remarks. Her cleaner, engaged in the first place 'to do the rough' had soon made it clear that she preferred polishing and cleaning silver to heavy work and her favorite tasks were those which kept her at a vantage point near one of the windows.

Now, having observed all there was to see in Orchard Drive, she had stationed herself at the french windows with the plate powder and a trayful of Susan's silver ornaments. It was half past nine. Although it had begun to rain, the drills had scarcely ceased in the past half-hour. Susan could hardly believe there was anything of interest to see from that window, but Mrs Dring kept craning her neck and pressing her face against the streaming glass until at last she said, 'They won't get no tea this morning.'

'Mmm?' Susan looked up from her typewriter.

'Them men. Look, he's going down the path now.' The summons couldn't be refused without rudeness. Susan joined her at the window. A tall workman in a duffel coat, its hood pulled up over his head, was making his way down Norths' garden from the back door towards the gate at the far end. 'I heard him banging on the back door. Wants his tea, I said to myself. Canteen's closed this morning, mate. Madam's got other things on her mind. Funny that dog of Winters didn't bark, though. Have they got it shut up for once?'

'No, it's out.'

It was raining steadily. The workman opened the gate. His companions were deep in their trench where one of them was still plying his drill. The solitary man warmed his hands at the bucket fire for a moment. Then he turned, his shoulders hunched, and strolled off along the road that skirted the cemetery.

Nodding her head grimly, Mrs Dring watched him disappear. 'Gone to fetch himself a cup from the café,' she said and added because Susan had retreated, 'Is the car still there?'

'Yes, it's still there.' The rain streamed down its closed windows and over the pale green bodywork. Someone else was looking at it, too, Eileen O'Donnell, who was putting up her umbrella after scuttling out of Louise's garden.

'Mrs O'Donnell's coming round to the back door, Mrs Dring,' Susan said. 'Just see what she wants, will you?'

She was sure she would be called to the conference that was about to ensue, but after a short conversation at the back door, Mrs Dring came back alone.

'Mrs North asked her to bring some fish fingers in for lunch in case her husband comes home. She says she's banged and banged at the front door but she can't make no one hear. She says the upstairs curtains are all drawn but that's on account of Mrs North not wanting the sun to fade the carpets. I reckon some folks go about with their eyes shut, don't know they're born. Sun, I said, what sun? A kid of five could tell you why she's drawn them curtains.'

Susan took the package, noting with amusement that it was wrapped in last week's edition of *Certainty*. How pained Julian would be! Its use as insulating material for frozen food was only one step up the scale from wrapping it round fish and chips.

'What am I supposed to do with them?'

'Mrs O'Donnell said you was going in there for coffee. And could you take them in with you just in case that poor wretch she's doing dirt to comes home for his lunch?'

But Susan had begun to doubt whether she was expected to keep that appointment. By the time Mrs Dring had finished the living-room and moved into what used to be Julian's study it was half past ten and the car was still outside. It looked as if Louise had forgotten. Love was generally supposed to conquer all and, although this was perhaps not what the adage meant, it certainly, in Susan's experience, banished from the lover's mind firm promises and prior engagements. Curious, though. Louise had been so insistent.

But between ten-thirty and eleven the time went slowly. There was no need to watch the window. The Airedale, now sheltering in Winters' porch, would warn her of the man's departure. Eleven struck and on the last stroke Susan's oppression lifted. The rain was fill-ing Monday's ruts with yellow clayey water, making pools round the wheels of the green car. Its driver was still inside Braeside and Susan sighed with relief. She wouldn't have to go now. There was no need for tact or kindness or firm advice because, by her own actions, Louise had cancelled the consultation.

Mrs Dring wrapped herself in a cocoon of blue polythene and trotted off into the rain, pausing to glower at the car and the curtained windows. Susan tried to remember how many times and for how long each time the car had been there before. Surely not more than three times and the man had never stayed as long as this. Didn't he have a job to go to? How could he afford to spend so much time—an entire morning—with Louise?

She opened the refrigerator door to make sandwiches for her lunch. The fish finger packet lay slightly askew on the metal slats. Did Bob ever come home to lunch? Eileen O'Donnell had seemed to think he might and now, as Susan considered, she remembered how Bob himself had told her he might come home one lunch-time.

Well, let him come home. Let him find them together. A showdown might be the best way out of this mess for all of them. But Susan took the packet from the refrigerator and went round to the front of the house from where she could see Braeside.

There was no one sitting in the through-room or in the little room at the other side of the front door. They must be still in the bedroom behind those closed curtains. Susan glanced at her watch and saw that it was gone half past twelve. How would she have felt if she had walked into that hotel, or wherever they had met, and found Julian in bed with Elizabeth? It would almost have killed her. Julian had been far more discreet than Louise—he was far cleverer—but still the process of discovery had been dreadfully painful to his wife. If Bob North came now it would be a far worse pain than that which would meet him.

That decided her. It was all very well deciding to

have as little as possible to do with the Norths. Circumstances altered cases and this was a hard case with circumstances as different from those of everyday life as Susan's present existence was from that of a year ago. She went back into the house and slipped her arms into the sleeves of her raincoat. Then she banged hard on Norths' front door, banged and rang the bell, but no one came. They must be asleep.

Reluctantly she went round to the side. What she was about to do would save Louise, at least for a time, from ignominy and possibly from violence, but Louise wouldn't be grateful. What woman would ever again be able to bear the sight of a neighbour who had found her in what the lawyers called *flagrante delicto*?

Better not to think about it. Get in, wake them up and go. Susan cared very little what Louise thought of her. She was going to give the Norths a very wide berth in future.

The back door was unlocked. If Louise was going to carry on with this sort of thing, Susan thought, she had a lot to learn. Julian would have made her a good adviser. The kitchen was untidy and freezing cold. Louise had stacked the breakfast things in the washing-up bowl but not washed them. There was a faint smell of cold fat from a water-filled frying-pan.

On the kitchen table stood the briefcase Susan had once or twice seen Louise's lover carrying up the path, and over the back of a chair was his raincoat. Susan put her package down and moved into the hall, calling Louise's name softly.

There was no answer, no sound from upstairs at all. In the little cloakroom a tap dripped. She came to the foot of the stairs and stood by the wall niche in which a plaster Madonna smiled down at her Child. It was grotesque.

No fires had been lighted in the house this morning and the ashes of yesterday's lay grey in the living-room hearth. All the windows streamed with water so that it was impossible to see out of them. Such heavy rain as this enclosed people like hibernating creatures, curled up dry, yet surrounded by walls of water. So it must have been for Louise and her lover, kissing, whispering, planning, while outside the rain fell and blotted out time.

Susan went upstairs. The bathroom door was open and the bathmat, a purple affair with a yellow scroll design in its centre, lay crookedly on the tiles. It looked as if none of the routine morning cleaning had been done. All the bedroom doors but one were open. She stood outside the closed door and listened.

Her reluctance to burst in on them had grown with every step and now she felt a strong revulsion. They might be naked. She put her hand to her forehead and felt a faint dew of sweat. It must be at least ten to one and Bob could be turning the corner of Orchard Drive at this moment.

She grasped the handle and opened the door gradually.

They were both on the bed, but the man appeared to be fully clothed. Only Louise's stockinged feet could be seen, for her lover lay spreadeagled across her, his arms and legs flung wide in the attitude of someone crucified on a St Andrew's Cross. His face was slightly turned as if he had fallen asleep with his lips pressed to Louise's cheek. They were both utterly still.

No one slept like that.

Susan came round the side of the bed between it and the dressing table and as she did so she stumbled over something hard and metallic that lay on the carpet. She looked down on it, breathing fast, and at first she thought it was a child's toy. But the Norths had no little boys to run up and down the stairs, shouting, Bang, bang, you're dead!

Momentarily she covered her face with her hands. Then she approached the bed and bent over the couple. One of Louise's shoulders was exposed. Susan touched it and the man's head lolled. Where his ear should have been was a neat round hole from which something sticky had run and dried. The movement revealed a mat of blood, liquid and caked, gumming their faces together and smothering the front of Louise's nightdress and housecoat.

Susan heard herself cry out. She put her hand up to her mouth and backed away, stumbling, while the floor eddied and rocked beneath her and the furniture swayed.

Chapter Six

The police asked her to wait there until they came. Susan's voice had shaken so much on the telephone that she was astonished she had made herself understood. She was almost numb with shock and long after the kind voice had stopped talking and told her to do nothing and to touch nothing, she sat staring at the Madonna while the receiver hung from her hand.

A rushing splash of water at the front of the house announced the arrival of the car. Susan was surprised she could stand. She made her way to the front door, clinging to the furniture and groping like a blind person.

The Airedale hadn't barked, but in her present state this didn't warn her. Then, in a kind of horror, she watched the latch turn from the inserted key.

Bob had come home to lunch.

He had dived through the rain from the newly serviced car to the door and he had stepped inside, shaking the drops from his hair, before he realised who waited for him in the cold shadowy hall.

'Susan?' She couldn't speak. Her lips parted, she drew a long breath. He looked at her, then past her at the dead ashes in the grate, the briefcase on the kitchen table. 'Where's Louise?'

Her voice came in a cracked whisper. 'Bob, I . . . She's upstairs. I . . . phoned the police.'

'Tell me what's happened?'

'She's dead. They're both dead.'

'You came to coffee,' he said stupidly and then he plunged for the stairs.

'You mustn't go up there!' Susan cried. She caught his shoulders and they were stiff, without a tremor, under her hands. He gripped her wrists as if to free himself and then the dog Pollux began to bark, dully at first, then furiously as the police car splashed through the puddles in the street. Bob dropped limply on to the stairs and sat with his head in his hands.

There were three policemen, a little brown-faced inspector called Ulph, a sergeant and a constable. They spent a long time upstairs and questioning Bob in the kitchen before they came to her. The sergeant passed the open living-room door with a sheaf of papers that looked like letters in his hand. Susan heard Bob say:

'I don't know who he is. I don't even know his name. Ask the neighbours. They'll tell you he was my wife's lover.' Susan shivered. She couldn't remember ever having felt so cold before. They were searching through the briefcase now. She could see them through the serving hatch and see Bob, sitting pale and stiff, by the table. 'No, I didn't know he was married,' Bob said. 'Why would I? Bernard Heller, did you say his name was? Of course I never ordered central heating.' His voice rose and cracked. 'Don't you understand? That was just a blind.'

'What about your own movements this morning, Mr North?'

'My car was in for a service. I left for work on foot. About half past eight. My wife was all right then. She was in her dressing-gown, making the bed, when I left. I'm a quantity surveyor and I went to Barnet to look at a building site. Then I collected my car from Harrow where it was being serviced and drove back here. I thought . . . I thought my wife was expecting me home for lunch.'

Susan turned her head away. The sergeant closed the door and the hatch. The coat Louise had worn the day before lay slung over the back of one of the chairs.

There was something very casual about that coat as if it had been put down only for a moment and any minute now Louise would come in and envelop her childish body in its comforting warmth. The tears came into Susan's eyes and she gave a little sob.

Upstairs the police were tramping heavily about. Then she heard someone descending the stairs and the small brown-faced inspector came in. He closed the door behind him and said gently to Susan, 'Try not to upset yourself, Mrs Townsend. I know this has been a great shock to you.'

'I'm quite all right, really. Only it's so cold in here.' He might think her eyes were watering from the cold, but she didn't think he would. He had compassionate eyes. Not the sort of policeman, she thought, who would be briskly hearty in the face of death or make jokes about it with his companions.

'Did you know Mrs North was on intimate terms with the man, Heller?' Inspector Ulph asked presently.

'I . . . Well, it was common knowledge,' Susan began. 'I know she was very unhappy about it. She was a Catholic and couldn't be divorced.' Her voice shook. 'She was terribly distressed when she came to see me yesterday.'

'Distressed to the point of taking her own life, or to agreeing to a suicide pact?'

'I don't know.' This sudden taking of responsibility frightened Susan. Her hands were icy cold and trembling. 'A Catholic wouldn't commit suicide, would she? But she was in a bad state. I remember thinking she was at the end of her tether.'

He asked her quietly about the events of the morning and Susan, trying to keep her voice steady, told him how she had seen Heller's car outside soon after nine; how she had waited and waited for Heller to leave; how Mrs O'Donnell had called and how, at last, she had come here to Braeside to alert Louise and Heller, believing them to be asleep.

'No one else came to this house during the morning?' Susan shook her head. 'Did you see anyone leave?'

'Only Mrs O'Donnell.'

'Well, that's all for now, Mrs Townsend. I'm afraid you'll have to be present at the inquest. Now, if I were you, I should telephone your husband and see if he can come home early. You shouldn't be alone.'

'I'm not married,' Susan said awkwardly. 'Well, that is, I'm divorced.'

Inspector Ulph made no reply to this, but he came with Susan to the door, lightly supporting her with one hand under her elbow.

As she came out into the garden, she blinked and started back. The crowd on the pavement affected her as bright sunlight shocks someone coming out of a dark room. Wrapped in coats, Doris and Betty and Eileen stood outside Doris's gate with the old woman who lived alone next to Betty, the bride from Shangri-La, the elderly couple from the corner house. Everyone who didn't go out to work was gathered there and everyone, their tongues stilled, was silent.

Even Pollux had been stunned into silence by those unprecedented comings and goings. He lay exhausted at his mistress's feet, his head between his paws.

The rain had ceased, leaving the roadway a glistening mirror of pools and wet tarmac. Raindrops dripped steadily from the cherry buds on to umbrellas and coat collars. Doris looked colder and more miserable than Susan had ever seen her, but for once she said nothing about the cold. She stepped forward, putting her arms around Susan's shoulders, and Inspector Ulph said:

'Will one of you ladies kindly look after Mrs Townsend?'

Susan let Doris lead her past the green Zephyr, the police car and the black mortuary van and into her own house. All the time she expected to hear her neighbours' chatter break out behind her, but there was only silence, a silence broken only by the steady drip-drip of water from the trees.

'I'll stay with you, Susan,' Doris said. 'I'll stay all

night. I won't leave you.' She didn't cite her nursing experience as qualification for this duty and she didn't clutch at the radiators. Her face was grey and huge-eyed. 'Oh, Susan, Susan . . . ! That man, did he kill her and himself?'

'I don't know. I think he must have.'

And the two women, friends only from propinquity and mutual practical need, clung together for a moment, their heads bowed on each other's shoulders.

It was curious, Susan thought, how tragedy seemed to bring out in everyone the best qualities, tact, kindness, sympathy. Afterwards the only really tactless action she could remember was the arrival of Roger Gibbs at Paul's party with the present of a toy revolver.

'I reckon some women are downright daft,' said Mrs Dring. 'Fancy, a gun! You'd think Mrs Gibbs'd have had more thought. And she's sent that boy of hers with a streaming cold. What'll I get them on playing? Musical Parcel? Squeak, Piggy, Squeak?'

Murder was the favourite party game among the under-tens in Orchard Drive. When no one suggested playing it, Susan knew they must have been forewarned by their mothers. Had those mothers told their sons what she had told Paul, that Mrs North had had an accident and been taken away? What do you tell someone who is old enough to wonder and be frightened but too young, far too young by years and years, to understand?

'I hope to God,' said Mrs Dring, 'young Paul won't have an accident with that watch his dad sent him.' She was unusually subdued this afternoon, softer-voiced and gentler, for all the dazzling aggressiveness of her red hair and the lilac suit she declared her husband had knitted. 'Has Mr Townsend been in touch yet?'

The watch had arrived by the first post and with it a card bearing a reproduction of Van Gogh's *Mills at Dordrecht*, a gloomy landscape that Julian had evidently preferred to the more suitable teddy-bear mouthing, 'Hallo, six-year-old'. He approved of culture being rammed home during the formative years. But there was no note inside for Susan and he hadn't phoned.

'He must have read about it,' said Doris indignantly, passing with a tray of sausage rolls.

Mrs Dring frowned at her. 'Perhaps he'll put something about it in his own paper.'

'It isn't that sort of paper,' said Susan.

It was only because she had wanted to keep Paul's interest from the tragedy next door that she had decided to go ahead with the party as planned. But now, as the little boys shouted and romped to the loud music from the record player, she wondered how much of this noise was reaching Bob. Since Louise and Heller had been found, he had only left Braeside for two visits to the police station. All the curtains, not just those upstairs, remained drawn. Gossip had reached the workmen on the cemetery road and today none of them had come up to the back door for their tea. Susan didn't care to think of Bob alone in there, living, moving, sleeping in the house where his wife had been shot. If he heard the children, would he take their merriment as the outward sign of her own indifference to his sorrow?

She hoped he wouldn't. She hoped he would understand and understand, too, that she hadn't yet called on him because she felt as yet he was better alone. That was why she hadn't been among the stream of tip-toeing housewives who knocked almost hourly at the Braeside door, some of them with flowers, some with covered baskets, as if he was ill instead of sick at heart.

Doris met Susan after the inquest was over and took her back for lunch in the over-heated room the Winters called their 'through-lounge'. An immense fire was burning. Susan saw that Doris's gentle, sympathetic mood had passed now. Her curiosity, her avidity for gossip, had returned, and, wondering if she was being just, Susan recognised in the huge fire, the carefully laid tray and the gloss of the room, a bait to keep her there for the afternoon, a festive preparation in return for which she must supply the hostess with every juicy tit-bit the inquest had afforded.

'Tell me about the gun,' Doris said, helping Susan plentifully to fruit salad.

'Apparently this man Heller smuggled it in from America. His twin brother was in court and he identified the gun and said Heller had tried to commit suicide in September. Not with the gun. The brother found him trying to gas himself.' Doris made eager encouraging noises. 'He shot poor Louise twice, both times through the heart, and then he shot himself. The pathologist thought it rather strange that he'd dropped the gun, but he'd known that to happen before in cases like this. They asked me if I'd heard the shots, but I hadn't.'

'You can't hear a thing when those drills are going.'

'I suppose that's why I didn't. The verdict was murder and suicide by Heller, by the way. Apparently he was always threatening suicide. His brother and his wife both said so.'

Doris helped herself to more salad, picking out pieces of pineapple. 'What was the wife like?'

'Rather beautiful, I thought. Only twenty-five.' Susan recalled how Carl Heller and Magdalene Heller had both tried to speak to Bob while they all waited for the inquest to begin and how Bob had turned from them, brushing off their overtures as if stung. She thought she would never forget how that big, heavy man had approached Bob and attempted to talk to him in his strongly accented English, and Bob's near-snarl, his bitter contempt for the woman whose dead husband had killed Louise. She wasn't going to tell Doris any of that, nothing of Bob's frenzied outburst in court when Magdalene Heller had accused him of driving his wife, through his own neglect, into another man's arms; nothing of the girl's stony, stunned horror that had broken at last into vituperative ravings at Bob.

'She knew about Louise,' Susan said, 'Heller had promised to give her up and try to patch up his marriage but he didn't keep his promise. He was miserable and suicidal about it. He'd been like that for months.'

'Had they ever met before, she and Bob?'

'Bob didn't even know Heller was married. No one knows how Louise and Heller met. Heller worked for a firm called *Equatair* and the managing director was in court. He said Heller was going as their representative to Zurich in May—apparently he'd always wanted to go back to Switzerland. He was born and brought up there—but he didn't show any interest when he was offered the post. I suppose he thought it would take him away from Louise. The managing director said *Equatair* got their custom by sending out business reply cards to people, but they hadn't sent one to Louise and everyone seemed to think Heller must have given her one just so that she could fill it in and arrange for him to call. That would make his visits look innocent, you see.'

Doris digested all this with satisfaction. She poked the fire until it crackled and blazed. Then she said, 'I wonder why they didn't just go away together?'

'I gathered from the letters that Heller wanted to but Louise wouldn't. It seemed as if Louise had never even told Bob about it, not in so many words.'

'Letters?' Doris said excitedly, discarding the rest of this fresh information. 'What letters?'

The police had found them in a drawer of Louise's dressing table, two love-letters from Heller to Louise which had been written in November and December of the previous year. Carl Heller had identified his brother's handwriting which, in any case, had been confirmed by an examination of Heller's work notes. When they were read in court Bob's face had grown grey and Heller's widow, covering her face with her hands, had buried her head in her brother-in-law's massive shoulder.

'They were just love-letters,' Susan said, sickened by this inquisition. 'They only read out bits.' Strange and horrible that they had picked out those bits which most cruelly maligned Bob. 'I can't remember what he'd written,' she lied.

Her expression must have shown her unwillingness to talk about it any more, for Doris, realising that she had gone as far as she dared, dropped the subject with a, 'It'll all be in the paper, I expect,' and suddenly became solicitous for Susan's welfare. 'I'm a beast, aren't I?' she said. 'Pestering you after all you've been through. You don't look at all well, as if you're sickening for something.'

'I'm all right.' In fact, Susan had begun to feel dizzy and rather sick. Probably it was only nerves and the hothouse temperature in this room. She would be better at home.

'Now I hope your place is really warm,' Doris twittered in the icy hall. 'I know it usually is. The great thing with shock and all this upheaveal is to keep in an even temperature.' She hunched her shoulders and wrapped her arms around her chest. 'An even temperature, that's one thing my sister tutor always impressed on me.'

For Susan's neighbours the inquest had been a kind of demarcation. It was over and with it most of the excitement, the terror and the scandal. Those involved and those looking on had reached a point at which they must again take up the strings of their lives. Susan had found two dead bodies, but Susan couldn't expect to be the centre of attraction, of sympathy and of comfort for ever.

But for all that, it gave her a slight shock to realise that Doris wasn't going to accompany her home. Mrs Dring had stayed with her last night, but she had said nothing about coming back. Quietly and as cheerfully as she could, Susan said good-bye to Doris and thanked her for lunch. Then she crossed the road, keeping her eyes averted from Braeside.

Work is generally recommended as the remedy for most ills and Susan went straight to her typewriter and Miss Willingale's manuscript. Her hands trembled and, although she flexed them and held them against the radiator, she found herself unable to type at all. Would she ever again be able to work in this house? It was so dreadfully like Braeside. With all her heart she wished she had minded her own business on Wednesday, even though that meant the discovery would have been Bob's and not hers.

Her first impression of it, her first sight of its interior, had left on her mind an image of a house of death and now her own, its facsimile, seemed contaminated. For the first time she wondered why she had ever stayed on here after her divorce. Like Braeside, it was a house where happy people had lived together and where that happiness had died away into misery. Now nothing remained of that happiness and there was nothing to replace it while these walls reflected back the sorrow they had seen.

Susan heard Bob's car come in but she couldn't look up. Now that it was all over, she might have been able to comfort him. He had needed a counsellor for loneliness and here she was, alone. She knew she had neither the physical strength nor the willpower to go out and knock on his door. It was a cold ugly place, this corner of suburbia, where a young man and a young woman could live next door to each other in identical houses, two walls only between them, yet be so bound by reticence and by convention that they could not reach out to each other in common humanity.

Many times she had cursed the daily arrival of Doris at teatime, but when Paul came in alone she missed her bitterly. A craving for company, stronger than she had felt for months, made her want to lie down and weep. A child of six, no matter how much beloved, is no company for a woman who feels as troubled and insecure as a child and Susan wondered if in her eyes he saw the same bewilderment, masked by a determined effort to make a brave show, as she saw in his.

'Roger Gibbs says Mrs North got shot by a man.' Paul said it quite casually, stretching his white face into a broad manly smile. 'And she was all over blood,' he said, 'and they had a trial like on the TV.'

Susan smiled back at him and her smile was as matter-of-fact, as bravely reassuring as his. In a light voice
she embarked on a bowdlerised explanation.

'He says this man wanted to marry her and he
couldn't, so he shot her. Why did he? He couldn't
marry her when she was dead. Daddy didn't shoot
Elizabeth and he wanted to marry her.'

'It wasn't quite the same. You'll understand when
you're older.'

'That's what you always say.' The smile had gone,
and with a quick glance at her, Paul went over to his
toy box. The gun Roger Gibbs had given him lay on
top of the little cars in their coloured boxes. He picked
it up, looked at it for a moment and then dropped it
listlessly. 'Can I wear my watch?' he said.

'Yes, darling, I suppose so.'

'Can I wear it right up until I go to bed?'

Susan heard Bob's car reverse out into the road.
This time she went to the window and watched him.
For a long time she stood there, staring at the empty
street and remembering how she had told him of her
loneliness on the night Julian had gone.

Chapter Seven

The inquest report was given a four-column
spread on an inside page of the *Evening Standard*.
David Chadwick bought a copy from a West End
newsvendor and, reading it as he went, strolled along
through the evening rush to where he had parked his
car some ten minutes' walk away. Wednesday's evening
paper had carried photographs of Magdalene Heller, of
Robert North and of the young woman, a neighbour,
who had found the bodies, but tonight there was only a
shot of Mrs. Heller leaving the court arm-in-arm with a
man. The caption said he was Bernard's twin brother
and from what David could see of him—his face and

the girl's were shielded by a magazine he was holding up—the resemblance between the brothers was striking.

It must be he for whom the slide projector had been borrowed. David had unwrapped it on Tuesday night, a little amused by the care Heller had taken of it, swaddling it in newspapers under its outer covering of brown paper. And then he hadn't been quite so amused, but moved and saddened. For one of the newspapers, some South London weekly, yellowed now and crumpled, contained a tiny paragraph reporting Heller's wedding to Miss Magdalene Chant. David only noticed it because the paragraph was ringed in ink and because Heller had written, just outside the ring, the date 7.6.62.

He had kept that paper as a souvenir, David thought, as simple people will. He had kept it until his marriage went wrong, until he had met Mrs North and wedding souvenirs were only a reminder of an encumbrance. So he had taken it, perhaps from a pile of other significant newspapers, and used it for wrapping someone else's property.

In the light of this notion and when he read of Heller's death, David had looked again at the sheets covering his projector and found, as he had suspected, newsprint commemorating Heller's success in some suburban swimming event and his inclusion among the guests at a darts club annual dinner. To Heller, evidently, these tiny claims to distinction, these printed chronicles, had once afforded the same pride as the record of his Order of Merit in *The Times* might give to a greater man. They had meant much and then suddenly, because his life had somersaulted and lost its meaning, they had meant nothing at all.

David thought of all this as he walked along Oxford Street and he thought also how strange it was that he, an acquaintance, merely, should have been with Heller on the eve of his death, should indeed have spent more time with him on that occasion than at any time during the two or three years since their first meeting. He wondered if he should have attended the inquest, but he could have told them nothing that was not already known. Now he asked himself, as men do under such circumstances, whether he had failed Heller in his last hours, if he could have shown more sympathy, and, worst of all, if there was any word he could have spoken of hope or encouragement that might have deflected the man from his purpose.

Who could tell? Who could have suspected what Heller had in mind? Nevertheless, David felt guilty and a sense of failure and inadequacy overcame him. He often thought of himself as a hesitant and indecisive person. Some men, hearty and brash perhaps but still the salt of the earth, would have sensed the depths of Heller's misery and, undeterred by his initial refusal to unburden his soul, have stayed and pumped his grief out of him. Others, the more sensitive of the do-gooders would have taken warning from that gun and linked its presence with Heller's confessed *weltschmerz*. He had done nothing, worse than nothing, for he had made his escape from that flat with obvious relief.

And on the next day Heller had shot himself. David felt bleakly depressed. He was driving, but he needed a drink, and all the breathalysers in the world could go to hell for all he cared. Folding the newspaper and cramming it into his pocket, he made for Soho and The Man in the Iron Mask.

It was early and the pub was nearly empty. David had never been there on a Friday before. He usually went home early on a Friday. Often he had a date and, anyway, to him the weekend started at five on Friday afternoon.

He didn't want to be alone yet and he looked around him to see if there was anyone here he knew well enough to sit with and talk to. But although all the faces were familiar, none was that of a friend. A man and a woman in their fifties were walking about, looking in silence at some new cartoons the licensee had pinned to the panelling; an elderly man who looked

like an out-of-work character actor sipped pernod at
the bar; the men with beards sat at a table near the pub
door. As he passed, David heard one of them say,
' "But that's share-pushing," I said in my naïve way.
"Call it what you like," he said, but he had a very
uneasy look on his face.'

'Quite,' said the other.

' "Some people will do anything for money," I said.
"Money's not everything." '

'That's a matter of opinion, Charles . . .'

The couple who had been looking at the cartoons sat
down and David saw that behind them, in the most
dimly lit corner, was a girl alone. Her back was turned
to him and she had only a blank wall to stare at. He
ordered a light ale.

'Buying on a margin like that,' said the man called
Charles. 'Apart from the ethics of the thing, I personally like to sleep quiet in my bed. Shall we go?'

'I'm ready when you are.'

They went and while David was waiting for his
change, he looked curiously at the solitary girl. He
could only see her back, made shapeless by the vinyl
jacket she wore, a head of glossy black hair, long legs
in velvet trousers twined round the legs of her chair.
She sat quite still, gazing at the brown panelling with
the raptness of someone watching an exciting television
programme.

He was surprised to see a girl in there alone. It used
to be the practice, a kind of unwritten law among West
End licensees, not to serve women on their own. Probably still was. However, this girl didn't seem to have a
drink.

There was something familiar about the set of her
shoulders and he was wondering whether he ought to
know her when the door opened to admit four or five
young men. The sudden cool draught caused her to
turn her head swiftly and nervously. Instantly, but almost incredulously, David recognised her.

'Good evening, Mrs Heller.'

The expression on her face was hard to analyse.

Fear? Caution? Dismay? Her curious green eyes, speckled with gold and iridescent like a fly's wing cases, flickered, then steadied. David wondered what on earth she could be up to, by herself in a West End pub on the very day of her dead husband's inquest.

'Is this your local or something?' she asked in a discouraging voice.

'I come here sometimes. Can I get you a drink?'

'No.' The negative exploded from her so loudly that several people turned to look. 'I mean, no, thanks. Don't bother. I'm just going.'

David had considered whether he ought to write her the conventional letter of condolence, but because offering sympathy to a woman released by death from an obviously unhappy marriage seemed misplaced, he had thought better of it. Now, however, he felt it incumbent on him to say something, if only to show he was aware of Heller's death, and he embarked on a little stilted speech of regret. But after murmuring, 'Yes, yes,' impatiently and nodding her head, she interrupted him inconsequentially.

'I was meeting someone, but she hasn't come.'

She? David thought of all the possible meeting places for two women in London in the evening. An office where the other girl worked? One of the shops that stayed open late? A café? A tube station? Never, surely, a pub in Soho. Magdalene Heller got up and began buttoning her coat.

'Can I take you to your station? My car's not far away.'

'Don't bother. It's not necessary.'

David drank up his beer. 'It's no bother.' he said. 'I'm sorry your friend didn't come.'

Politeness wasn't her strong suit, but in everyone except the savage, convention forbids actually running from an acquaintance and slamming the door in his face. That, he thought, was what she would like to have done.

They approached the door and she fumbled in her bag with fingers he thought none too steady. The cigarette was eventually found. David got out his lighter and held the flame up to her face.

Behind her the door opened. It opened perhaps a foot and then stuck. Magdalene Heller inhaled, turning her head. David didn't know why he kept his finger pressed on the light, the flame still flaring. The man who had opened the door stood on the step, staring in.

Again Magdalene Heller faced him. Her lips parted and she said with an unexpected effusiveness, 'Thank you so much, David. I'm glad we ran into each other.'

David was so taken aback by his sudden *volte-face* that he too stared into her beautiful, suddenly flushed face. Her cigarette had gone out. He lit it again. The man backed abruptly the way he had come, leaving the door swinging.

They were ready to go, on the point of leaving, but she opened her bag again, rummaging aimlessly in its contents.

'D'you know that fellow?' David asked and then, feeling that he had been rude, added truthfully, 'I'm sure I do. Might be someone I've come into contact with on television, of course. His face seemed awfully familiar.'

'I didn't notice.'

'Or I could have seen his picture in the newspaper. That's it, I think, in connection with some case or other.'

'More likely on TV,' she said casually.

'He seemed to know you.'

Or had it been that this girl was so outstandingly good-looking that even in the West End where beauty is common, men stared at her? She put her hand on his arm. 'David?' She was lovely, the face close to his as they came into the street, flawless with its orchid skin and gold-speckled eyes. Why then did her touch affect him strangely, almost as if a snake had flickered against his sleeve? 'David, if you haven't anything better to do, would you—would you drive me home?'

All the way to the car she chattered feverishly and she

clung to David's arm. She had an accent, he noticed, that wasn't from London or from the North. He couldn't quite place it, although he tried while he pretended to listen to what she was saying, whether she would be able to keep her flat, her future, her lack of training for any sort of job.

She didn't look like a new widow. The clothes she was wearing were not those he had seen in the inquest report picture, although those had been indecorous enough. Now she was dressed shabbily, casually and—he observed this for the first time as she got into the car—provocatively. He disliked fly-fronted trousers on women and these were far too tight. She took off her shiny jacket and draped it over the seat. Her breasts, though undoubtedly real, had an inflated rubbery look and they were hoisted so high as to suggest discomfort, but as if the discomfort were worth suffering for the sake of the erotic appeal. All this was fair enough in a beautiful girl of twenty-five, all this sticky seductive make-up, long cheek-enveloping hair, and emphasis given to a bold figure. But she wasn't just a girl of twenty-five. She was a widow who that morning had attended the inquest on her husband and who was supposed to be, if not grief-stricken, stunned by shock and subdued by care.

They had been driving along for perhaps a quarter of an hour when she put her hand on his knee. He hadn't the courage to remove it and he began to sweat when the fingers caressed and kneaded his flesh. She smoked continuously, opening the window every couple of minutes to flick ash out into the street.

'Is it straight on,' he said, 'or left here?'

'You can take the back doubles. It's shorter.' She wound down the window and threw her cigarette-end on to the pavement, narrowly missing a little Chinese. 'Take the next exit. I'll navigate for you.'

David obeyed her, going left, right, left again, and plunging into a web of mean streets. It was still quite light. They came to a bridge with huge concrete pillars at either end, carved columns vaguely Egyptian, that might have come from the Valley of the Kings. Underneath was a kind of marshalling yard, overlooked by factories and tower blocks.

'Down here,' Magdalene Heller said. It was a narrow street of tiny slum houses. Ahead he could see a tall chimney, a gasometer. 'What's the hurry?'

'It's not exactly a beauty spot, is it? Not the sort of place one wants to hang about in.'

She sighed, then touched his hand lightly with one fingertip. 'Would you stop a moment, David? I have to get cigarettes.'

Why couldn't she have bought them in London? Anyway, the three or four she had smoked had come from a nearly full pack. He could see a shop on the corner and he could see that it was closed.

Reluctantly he pulled into the kerb. They were quite alone and unobserved. 'I'm so lonely, David,' she said. 'Be nice to me.' Her face was close to his and he could see every pore in that smooth fungoid skin, mushroom skin, rubbery as he could guess that too-perfect, pneumatic body to be. There was a highlight on her lips where she had licked them. 'Oh, David,' she whispered.

It was like a dream, a nightmare. It couldn't be happening. As if in a nightmare, for a moment he was stiff and powerless. She touched his cheek, stroking it, then curled her warm hands around his neck. He told himself that he had been wrong about her, that she was desperately lonely, devastated, longing for comfort, so he put his arms around her. The full wet lips he bypassed, pressing his cheek against hers.

He stayed like that for perhaps thirty seconds, but when her mouth closed on his neck with a sea-anemone suction, he took his arms from her shoulders.

'Come on,' he said. 'People can see us.' There was no one to see. 'Let's get you home, shall we?' He had to prise her off him, a new and quelling experience. She was breathing heavily and her eyes were sullen. Her mouth drooped pathetically.

'Come and have a meal with me,' she said. Her voice had a dismayed whine in it. 'Please do. I can cook for you. I'm a good cook, really I am. You mustn't judge by what I was giving Bernard that night. He didn't care what he ate.'

'I can't, Magdalene.' He was too embarrassed to look at her.

'But you've come all this way. I want to talk to you.' Incredibly, the hand came back to his knee. 'Don't leave me all alone.'

He didn't know what to do. On the one hand, she was a widow, young, poor, her husband dead only two days before. No decent man could abandon her. He had already abandoned the husband, and the husband had killed himself. But on the other hand, there was her outrageous behaviour, the clumsy seduction attempt. There was nothing cynical in concluding her offer of a meal was just eyewash. But was he justified in leaving her? He was a grown man, reasonably experienced; he could protect himself, and under the peculiar circumstances, do so with tact. Above all, he wondered why he need protect himself. Was she a nymphomaniac, or so unhinged by shock as to be on the edge of a mental breakdown? He wasn't so vain as to suppose against all previous evidence to the contrary, that women were spontaneously and violently attracted to him. The wild notion that he might suddenly have developed an irresistible sex appeal crossed his mind to be immediately dismissed as fantastic.

'I don't know, Magdalene,' he said doubtfully. They passed the prison or barrack wall and they passed the lighted cinema. There was a long bus queue at the stop by the park. David heard himself let out a small sound, a gasp, a stifled exclamation. His hands went damp and slithered on the wheel. Bernard Heller stood at the tail of the queue, reading his evening paper.

Of course, it wasn't Bernard. This man was even bigger and heavier, his face more ox-like, less intelligent than Bernard's. If David hadn't already been jumpy and bewildered he would have known at once it was the twin brother, Carl who had borrowed the slide projector.

But they were uncannily alike. The resemblance made David feel a bit sick.

He pulled the car in alongside the queue and Carl Heller lumbered into the back. Magdalene had gone rather pale. She introduced them snappily, her accent more pronounced.

'David's going to have dinner with me, Carl.' She added as if she had a part-share in the car and more than a part-share in David, 'We'll drop you off first.'

'I can't stay for dinner, Magdalene,' David said firmly. The presence of Bernard's twin both discomfited him and gave him strength. Here were capable hands in which he could safely leave the girl. 'I'm afraid I don't know where you live.'

Magdalene said something that sounded like Copenhagen Street and she had begun on a spate of directions when David felt a heavy hand, grotesquely like the comedy scene hand of the law, lower itself on to his shoulder and rest there.

'She's in no fit state for company tonight, Mr Chadwick.' The voice was more guttural than Bernard's. There was more in that sentence than a polite way of telling someone he wasn't wanted. David heard in it self-appointed ownership, pride, sorrow and—yes, perhaps jealousy. 'I'll look after her,' Carl said. 'That's what my poor brother would have wanted. She's had a bad day, but she's got me.'

David thought he had never heard anyone speak so ponderously, so slowly. The English was correct and idiomatic, yet it sounded like a still difficult foreign tongue. You would grow so bored, exasperated even, if you had to listen to this man talking for long.

Magdalene had given up. She said no more until they reached Hengist House. Whatever she had been trying on, she had given it up.

'Thanks for the lift.'

'I'm glad I saw you,' David said untruthfully. Carl's face was Bernard's, unbearably pathetic, dull with grief, and David heard himself say in a useless echo of his words to the dead man, 'Look, if there's anything I can do . . .'

'No one can do anything.' The same answer, the same tone. Then Carl said, 'Time will do it.'

Magdalene lagged back. 'Good night, then,' David said. He watched Carl take her arm, propelling her, while she tugged a little and looked back, like a child whose father has come to fetch it home from a dangerous game with the boy next door.

Chapter Eight

Julian and Susan had tried to be very civilised and enlightened. They had to meet for Julian to see his son. It had seemed wiser to try to maintain an unemotional friendship and Susan had known this would be difficult. How difficult, how nearly impossible, she hadn't envisaged. When life went smoothly, she preferred not to be reminded of Julian's existence and his telephone calls—incongruously more frequent at such times—were an uncomfortable disruption of peace. But when she was unhappy or nervous she expected him to know it and to a certain degree be a husband to her again, as if he were in fact a husband separated from his wife for perhaps business reasons, who had to live far away.

She knew this was an impossible hope, totally unreasonable. Nothing on earth would have made her disclose this feeling to anyone else. Julian had his own life to lead.

But was it so unreasonable to expect at this time some sign of concern from him? Louise's death had been in all the newspapers; tonight both evening papers featured the inquest. Julian was an avid reader of newspapers and the fact that the two Evenings had been delivered to her house, were now spread on the table before her, was a hangover from her marriage to Julian who expected his wife to be well-informed.

That he still hadn't phoned showed a careless disregard for her that changed her loneliness from a gathering depression to a panicky terror that no one in the world cared whether she lived or died. To spend the evening and night alone here suddenly seemed a worse ordeal to pass through than any she had encountered since her divorce. For the first time she resented Paul. But for him, she could have gone out tonight, gone to the pictures, rooted out a friend from the past. Here in this house there was nothing else to think about but Louise and the only conversation possible an interchange between herself and her *alter ego*. The sentences almost spoke themselves aloud, the answerless questions. Could she have helped? Could she have changed the course of things? How was she going to stand days, weeks, months of this house? Above all, how to cope with Paul?

He had gone on and on that evening about Louise and the man. Because someone had told him Louise had loved this man, he found curious childish parallels between her case and that of his parents. Susan too had found parallels and she couldn't answer him. She reproached herself for her inadequacy but she was glad when at last he fell silent and slid the beloved cars out of their boxes, playing with absorption until bedtime.

So it was unforgivable to feel this mounting anger when she went to her desk and saw how he had left it, a multi-storied car park with miniscule bonnet and fender protruding from every slot and cranny. Black tyre marks were scored across each of the top three sheets of her typescript. Unforgivable to be angry, cruel perhaps not to control that anger.

But the words were out when she was halfway up the stairs, before she could stop herself and count to ten through set teeth.

'How many times have I told you to leave my things alone? You're never to do it again, never! If you do, I won't let you wear your watch for a whole week.'

Paul gave a heart-breaking wail. He made a grab for the watch, pulling it from its velvet-lined case, and cradling it against his face. Desperately near tears herself, Susan fell on her knees beside him and took him in her arms.

'Stop crying. You mustn't cry.'

'I'll never do it again, only you're not to take my watch.' How quickly a child's tears evaporated! They left no trace, no ugly swollen redness. Louise's weeping had left her face furrowed, old, distraught.

Paul watched her with a child's sharp intuition. 'I can't go to sleep, Mummy,' he said. 'I don't like this house any more.' His voice was small and muffled against her shoulder. 'Will they catch the man and put him in prison?'

'He's dead too, darling.'

'Are you sure? Roger's mother said he'd gone away, but she said Mrs North had gone away too. Suppose he isn't dead and he comes back here?'

Susan left the light on in his bedroom and the light on on the landing. When she got downstairs again she lit the twentieth cigarette of the day, but the smoke seemed to choke her, starting a long spasm of coughing. It left her shivering with cold. She ground out the cigarette, turned up the central heating and, going to the phone, dialled Julian's number.

Tonight, when nothing went right and all things seemed antagonistic, it would have to be Elizabeth who answered.

'Hallo, Elizabeth. Susan.'

'Susan . . .' The echoed name hung in the air. As always, Elizabeth's gruff schoolgirlish voice held a note of doubt. The impression was that she knew quite ten Susans, all of whom were likely to telephone her and announce themselves without surname or other qualification.

'Susan Townsend.' It was grotesque, almost past bearing. 'May I have a word with Julian?'

'Sure, if you want. He's just finishing his mousse.' How those two harped on food! They had plenty in common; one day, no doubt, they would share obesity. 'Good thing you rang now. We're just off for our week-end with Mummy.'

'Have a good time.'

'We always have a great time with Mummy. I do think all this killing in Matchdown Park is the end, and you up to your neck in it. But I expect you kept cool. You always do, don't you? I'll just fetch Julian.'

He sounded as if his mouth was full.

'How are you, Julian?'

'I am well.'

Susan wondered if her sigh of exasperation was audible at the other end. 'Julian, I expect you've read about all this business out here. What I want to ask you is, d'you mind if we sell this house? I want to move as soon as possible. I can't remember the way our joint property is tied up but I know it's complicated and we both have to agree.'

'You must do exactly as you like, my dear.' Had he brought the mousse with him? It sounded as if he was eating while he talked. 'You're absolutely free. I shan't interfere at all. Only don't think of taking less than ten thousand and wherever you choose to make your new home, see it's within distance of a decent school for my son and a good prep school when the time comes.' He swallowed and said breezily, 'Just put it in some agent's hands and let him do the lot. And if I meet anyone pining to vegetate in salubrious Matchdown Park I'll send him along. Tell me, were we ever on more than nodding terms with these Norths?'

'You weren't on more than nodding terms with anyone. Sneering terms might be more accurate.'

For a moment she thought he was offended. Then he said, 'You know, Susan, you've got a lot more waspish since we parted. It's rather becoming, almost makes me . . . well, no, I won't say that. Rather a sexy-looking fellow, this North, as I recall, and a quasi-professional job, surely?'

'He's a quantity surveyor.'

'Whatever that may be. I suppose you and he are

living in each other's pockets now, popping in and out of each other's houses. No wonder you want to move.'

'I don't imagine I shall ever speak to him again,' said Susan. Julian muttered something about finishing dinner, packing, setting off for Lady Maskell's. She said good-bye quickly because she knew she was going to cry. The tears rolled down her cheeks and she didn't bother to wipe them away. Every time Julian talked to her she hoped for kindness and consideration, forgetting for the moment that this was how he had always spoken to other people, waspishly, lightly, frivolously. She was the other people now and the tender kindness was Elizabeth's.

And yet she didn't love him any more. It was the habit of being a wife, of coming in a man's scheme of things, that she missed. When you were married you couldn't ever be quite alone. You might be on your own which was different. And whoever she begged to come to her now would look on her necessarily as a nuisance, a bore that separated them from the person they would prefer to be with.

For all that, she considered phoning Doris or even Mrs Dring. Her pride prevented her as her fingers inched towards the receiver.

Paul had fallen asleep. She covered him up, washed and redid her face. There was no point in it, but she sensed that if she were to go to bed now, at seven-thirty, it might become a precedent. You went to bed early because there was nothing to stay up for. You lay in bed late because getting up meant facing life.

She was going to move. Cling on to that, she thought, cling on to that. Never again to see the cherry trees coming into crêpe paper bloom, the elms swaying above the cemetery, the three dull red pinpoints burning by the roadworks trench. Never again to run to a window because a dog barked or watch Bob North's headlights swing across the ceiling and die in a wobble of shadow against the wall.

They were glazing through the room now. Susan pulled the curtains across. She opened a new packet of cigarettes and this time the smoke didn't make her cough. Her throat felt dry and rough. That must be the intense heat. Why did she keep feeling alternately cold and hot? She went outside to adjust the heating once more, but stopped, jumping absurdly with shock, when the front door bell rang.

Who would call on her at this hour? Not surely those friends of her marriage, Dian, Greg, Minta, their consciences alerted by the evening papers? The dog hadn't barked. It must be Betty or Doris.

The man on the doorstep cleared his throat as she put her hand to the latch. The sound, nervous, gruff, diffident, told her who it was before she opened the door. She felt an unpleasant thrill of trepidation that melted quickly into pure relief that anyone at all had come to call on her. Then, coughing again, as nervous as he, she let Bob North in.

At once he made it clear that this wasn't a mere doorstep call and Susan, who had told Julian she would probably never be on more than remote terms with her neighbour, was curiously glad when he walked straight into the living-room as if he were a friend and a regular visitor. Then she told herself with self-reproach, that Bob had far more cause to be lonely and unhappy than she.

His face now bore no sign of the misery and bitterness to which he had given vent in court and although he again apologised for Susan's involvement in his affairs, he said nothing of why he had come. Susan had already put her sympathy and her sorrow for him into awkward words and now she could find nothing to say. That he had come with definite purpose was made clear by his nervous manner and the narrow calculating look he gave her as they faced each other in the warm untidy room.

'Were you busy? Am I interrupting something?'

'Of course not.' His loss made him different from other men, a pariah, someone you had to treat warily, yet appear to be no different. She wanted to behave both as if the tragedy had never happened and at the same time as if he were deserving of the most solicitous consideration. And odd reflection came to her, that it was impossible to feel much pity for anyone as good-looking as Bob. His appearance called for envy from men and a peculiarly humiliating admiration from women. If the tragedy hadn't happened and he had called like this, she would have felt ill-at-ease alone with him.

'Won't you sit down?' she said stiffly. 'Can I get you a drink?'

'That's very sweet of you.' He took the bottle and the glasses from her. 'Let me.' She watched him pour gin into a glass and fill it high with bitter lemon. 'What can I get you? No, don't shake your head . . .' He gave a very faint crooked grin, the first smile she had seen on his face since Louise's death. 'This is going to be a long session, Susan, if you'll bear with me.'

'Of course,' she murmured. This, then, was the purpose of his visit, to talk to one near enough to listen, far enough to discard when the unburdening was complete. Louise had tried to do the same, Louise had died first. Somewhere in all this there was a curious irony. Bob's dark blue eyes were on her, fixed, cool, yet doubtful as if he had still a choice to make and wondered whether he was choosing wisely.

She moved away from him to sit down and the sofa suddenly seemed peculiarly soft and yielding. A moment ago she had been glad to see Bob; now she felt only deeply tired. Bob walked the length of the room, turned sharply and, taking a roll of paper from his pocket, dropped it on the coffee table between them. He had an actor's grace, an actor's way of moving because he had studied and learnt those movements. Susan thought this with slight surprise and then she wondered if his gestures looked calculated because he was keeping them under a painful control.

She reached for the papers, raising her eyebrows at him. He nodded sharply at her. Could these quarto sheets be connected with some legal business? Could they even possibly be Louise's will?

Susan unfolded the first page without much curiosity. Then she dropped it with a sharp exclamation as if it had been rolled round something red hot or something slimily disgusting.

'No, I can't possibly! I can't read these letters!'

'You recognise them, then?'

'Parts of them were read in court.' Susan's face burned. 'Why ...' She cleared her throat which had begun to feel sore and swollen. 'Why do you want me to read them?' she asked fiercely.

'Don't be harsh with me, Susan.' His brow puckered like a little boy's. She thought suddenly of Paul. 'The police gave me these letters. They *belonged* to Louise, you see, and I've—well, I've inherited them. Heller sent them to her last year. *Last year,* Susan. Since I read them, I haven't been able to think of anything else. They haunt me.'

'Burn them.'

'I can't. I keep on reading them. They've poisoned every happy memory I have of her.' He put his face in his hands. 'She wanted to be rid of me. I was just an encumbrance. Am I so loathsome?'

She avoided the direct answer, for the question was absurd. It was as if a millionaire had asked for her opinion on the low state of his finances. 'You're overwrought, Bob. That's only natural. When people are having a love affair, they say things they don't mean, things that aren't true, anyway. I expect Julian's wife said a lot of exaggerated unpleasant things about me.' She had never considered this before. It cost her an effort to put it into words.

He nodded eagerly. 'That's why I came to you. I knew you'd understand.' Swiftly he got up. The letters were written on stiff quarto-size paper and they had once again sprung back into a roll. He flattened them with the heel of his hand and thrust them at Susan, holding them a few inches from her face.

She had spoken of the possibility of Elizabeth's having written defamatory things about her. If this had happened and such a letter come into her possession, nothing would have induced her to show it to a stranger. And yet the majority of strangers would jump at the chance. She must be exceptionally squeamish or perhaps just a coward, an ostrich. How avidly Doris, for instance, would scramble to devour Heller's words if, instead of coming here, Bob were baring his soul in the house across the street!

Susan reached for a cigarette. The thought came to her that she had never read a love-letter. During their courtship she and Julian had seldom been separated and when they were they phoned each other. Certainly she had never read anyone else's. Bob, who valued her for her experience, would be astonished at such innocence.

Perhaps it was this innocence that still held her back. Louise's love affair, a housewife and a salesman, a hole-in-the-corner ugliness, seemed to her merely sordid, unredeemed by real passion. The letters might be obscene. She glanced up at Bob and suddenly she was sure he would expose her to nothing disgusting. With a little sigh, she brought Heller's looped sloping writing into focus, the address: Three, Hengist House, East Mulvihill, S.E.29, the date, November 6th, '67, and then she began to read.

My darling,
    You are in my thoughts night and day. Indeed, I do not know where dreaming ends and waking begins, for you fill my mind and I go about in a daze. I am a bit of a slow stupid fellow at the best of times, sweetheart—I can picture you smiling at this and maybe (I hope) denying it—but it is true and now I am half-blind and deaf as well. My love for you has made me blind, but I am not so blind that I cannot see into the future. It frightens me when I think we may have to go on like this for years, only seeing each other occasionally and then for a few snatched hours.

Why won't you make up your mind to tell him? It's no good saying something may happen to make everything come right for us. What can happen? He is not an old man and may live for years and years. I know you say you don't wish him dead but I can't believe it. Everything you say and the very look on your face shows me you feel he's just a burden to you. The rest is superstition and in your heart you know it. He has no rights, no hold over you that anyone would recognise these days.

What it boils down to, what you're really saying is that we just have to hang on and wait till he dies. No, I'm not trying to persuade you to put something in his tea. I'm telling you for the hundredth time to make him understand you have a right to your own life, to take it from him and give it to your loving but very miserable,

Bernard

No, it wasn't a disgusting letter—unless you happened to know the man Heller referred to as a tiresome encumbrance. And if you didn't know the man, you might even find the second letter poignant. If you didn't know the man and hadn't lived next door to the wife from whose betrayal Heller had drawn his insinuations.

The address was the same, the date nearly a month later. December 2nd, '67, Susan read, and then:

My sweet darling,

I can't go on living without you. I can't go on existing and working miles away from you, thinking of you with him and wasting your life being a slave to him. You must tell him about me, that you have found someone who really loves you and will give you a proper home at last. You half promised you would when we met last week, but I know how weak you can be when actually with him.

Does he really need all this care and attention and wouldn't a housekeeper be able to do everything you do now? He has always been harsh and ungrateful, God knows, and you say sometimes violent. Tell him tonight, darling, while you are with him in what I can only call your prison.

Time goes on so quickly (it seems slow to me now but I know it really flies) and what will you be like in a few years time, growing older and still tied to him? He will never come to appreciate and love you now. All he wants is a servant. You will be bitter and soured, and do you really think our love can still last under those conditions? As for me, I sometimes think that without you I can only make an end to myself. I just can't envisage life dragging on like this much longer.

Write to me or, better still, come to me. You have never seen me happy yet, not happy as I will be when I know you have left him at last.

Bernard

Susan folded the letters and they stared at each other in a deep, sickened silence. To break it, she shied away from touching on the emotional content of the letters and, seizing on something mundane said, 'Were there only these? Didn't he write any more?'

'Aren't they sufficient?'

'I didn't mean that. Only that I should have expected more, a whole series.'

'If there were more, she didn't keep them.'

'She may have been ashamed of them,' Susan said bitterly. 'They aren't exactly couched in deathless prose, not literary gems.'

'I hadn't noticed. I'm no judge of that sort of thing. Their meaning is clear enough. Louise hated me so much she was prepared to tell any lies about me.' He took the letters from her hand and kept hold of the hand, clutching it sexlessly, desperately, like a lifeline. 'Susan,' he said, 'you don't believe it, do you, that I was a violent, harsh, slave-driver?'

'Of course I don't. That's why I don't think there's any point in keeping the wretched things. You'll only read and re-read them and torture yourself.'

For a dreadful moment she thought he was going to cry. His face twisted and it was almost ugly. 'I can't bring myself to destroy them,' he said. 'Susan, would you do it, would you—if I left them here?'

Slowly she took them from his lap, expecting her wrist to be seized again. She felt rather as she did when each night she surreptitiously slipped the watch from Paul's hands while he slept. Here was the same held-breath caution, the same fear of a cry of protest. But Paul loved his watch. Was a kind of love curiously combined with Bob's hatred of these letters?

He let her take them. 'I promise, Bob,' she said, and a trembling weariness washed over her. 'I promise, as soon as you've gone.'

She thought he would go then. It was still early, but she had forgotten about precedents, about giving in to depression and tiredness. Now she only wanted to sleep.

But, 'I ought not to bore you with all this,' he said in the tone of someone who has every intention of doing so. Evidently her tiredness didn't show. 'I've got to talk to someone. I can't bear to keep it all to myself.'

'Go ahead, Bob. I understand.'

She she listened while he talked of his marriage, his once great love for Louise, their disappointment at their childlessness. He speculated as to where Louise and Heller had met, what they could have had in common and how strange it was that Louise's faith had deserted her. He spoke with violence, with passion, with incredulity and once he got up to pace the room. But instead of exhausting him as they exhausted Susan, his outbursts seemed to invigorate him. Cleansed and renewed, he talked for half an hour, while Susan lay back, nodding sometimes and assuring him of her sympathy. The stubs in her ashtray piled up until they looked like the poster picture in the doctor's surgery. Her throat had become rasping, rubbing sandpaper.

'My God, I'm sorry, Susan,' he said at last. 'I've worn you out. I'll go.' She was beyond polite dissuasion. He took her hands impulsively and as he bent over her his dark vivid face went out of focus and swam above her. 'Promise I'll never see those foul things again,' he said. She nodded. 'I'll let myself out. I'll never forget what you've done for me.'

The front door closed and the sound of its closing reverberated in her head to settle into a steady throbbing. Long shivers were coursing through her now and her back had begun to ache. She closed her eyes and saw Bob's face suspended before them. Heller's spidery writing danced and the beating in a corner of her brain became the sharp clicking of Louise's heels.

When she awoke it was midnight. The air was foul with smoke. The heating had shut itself off and it was the cold which had awakened her, eating into her bones. Sometime before she slept she must have taken the glasses to the kitchen and emptied that spilling ashtray. She remembered nothing about it, but as she staggered to her feet she knew very well that her inertia and the sharp pain in her throat had little to do with the emotional vicissitudes of the day.

Symptoms like these had real physical cause. She had the flu.

Chapter Nine

Since Julian's departure Susan had slept in one of the two spare bedrooms at the back of the house. It was a small room with a north light but now she was glad she had chosen it. To be ill in a bedroom that was the twin of Louise's bedroom, to lie in a bed placed just where hers was, was the worst medicine Susan could think of.

She had passed a miserable night, getting sleep only in short snatches. By morning the bed was piled with every surplus blanket in the house, although Susan only dimly remembered fetching the extra ones. She took her temperature and found it was a hundred and three.

'Go over to Mrs Winter, darling,' she said when Paul pottered in at eight. 'Ask her to give you breakfast.'

'What's the matter with you?'

'I've just got a bad cold.'

'I expect you caught it off Roger Gibbs at the party,' said Paul, adding as if praising a friend for a remarkable altruism. 'He gives his colds to everyone.'

The doctor came, arriving simultaneously with Doris who stood at the end of the bed, confirming his diagnosis and chipping in every few seconds with suggestions of her own.

'I don't want you to catch it, Doris,' Susan said feebly after he had gone.

'Oh, I shan't catch it. I never catch things.'

It was true. For all her vulnerability to low temperatures and her huddling into cardigans, Doris never even had a cold. 'I got immune to all that in my nursing days,' she said, punching pillows like a boxer. 'Just listen to my dog. He's kicking up a racket because all the funeral cars have come next door.' Cocking her head, she listened to the distant barking and what might have been an undertaker's subdued football. 'One thing, I've got an excuse for not going and it'd be suicide for you to get up.' She clapped her hand over her mouth. 'Oh dear, that's a dirty word round here, isn't it? I've heard the Catholics won't have Louise in their cemetery. Shame, really, when it was Heller who did it.' The dog barked hollowly, a door slammed. 'I've seen Bob and he sent his best wishes for a speedy recovery. Fancy, with all his troubles, he wanted to know if there was anything he could do. I said to John, Bob North's got a terrific admiration for Susan in his way, and John agreed with me. I've turned your heating full on, my dear. I hope you don't mind, but you know what a chilly mortal I am. I wonder if he'll get married again.'

'Who?'

'Bob, of course. Well, marriage is a habit, isn't it, and I should think it would be funny adapting yourself to the single life. Oh God, there I go again, both feet in it!' Doris blushed and hugged herself in her big double-knit jacket. 'Could you eat a cut off the joint? No, better not. By the way, I tidied up for you and dusted through. Not that it needed it, it was all as neat as a pin.'

'You're being awfully kind.'

'Just bossy and managing, lovey.' Doris's sudden unexpected self-analysis endeared her to Susan more than all her expert attention. She wished her painful throat and her huge weariness would allow her to speak her gratitude. She croaked out something about Paul and Doris said, 'He's gone with Richard. You can leave him with us for the weekend. What are you going to do with yourself? Maybe we could have the telly fetched up here.'

'No, really, Doris. I might read a bit later on.'

'Well, if you get bored, you can always watch the workmen slogging themselves to death.' And, twitching the curtains, Doris laughed loudly. 'They're as bad as I am, must have their fire and their tea.'

Watching three workmen fill in a trench and dig another one six feet up the road would hardly have been Susan's idea of compelling entertainment when she was well. She had often thought, as most people do, that if she was ever confined to bed, mildly sick, she would use the time to read one of those classics that demand uninterrupted concentration. So when Doris returned at lunchtime she asked her to fetch *Remembrance of Things Past* from the collection of books Julian had left behind him.

But Proust defeated her. She was uninterrupted, but her powers of concentration were so diminished as to leave her mind a vague blur of half-remembered worries, disjointed fears and thoughts of her removal from Matchdown Park. She put the book down after ten minutes of peering at the dancing print and, impatient to find herself yielding to Doris's silly suggestion, turned her eyes to the window.

The sky was a pale cloudy blue across which the elm branches spread their black lace tracery. She could just see the sun, a yellow puddle in the clouds. It all looked dreadfully cold and she could understand the workmen's need of a fire. The three of them were standing round it now, stirring tea in mugs Susan could see were coarse and cracked. Louise had given them china cups with saucers.

She propped the pillows behind her so that she could see better. Oddly enough, there was something peculiarly diverting in watching three unknown people moving about and talking to each other. That she couldn't hear what they said only increased the piquancy. There was an oldish man, a younger man and a boy. The two older men seemed to be chaffing the boy, but he took their shoving and their laughter good-humouredly. It was his task to collect the three mugs and take them back into the shelter of the hut. Susan saw him shake the dregs on to the clay-plastered pavement and wipe the insides of the mugs out with newspaper.

Presently they clambered back into their trench and the old man bowed his body over the broad handle of the drill. The boy had got hold of a muddy tangle of cables and capered about with them at which his companion started a mock fight. Only their heads and their flailing hands were visible over the ridge of the trench, but the boy's laughter was so shrill that, far away as she was, Susan could hear it above the reverberations of the drill.

Then a girl in a short red coat appeared around the corner of O'Donnells' fence and immediately, ceasing their sparring, the two younger men whistled her. She had to pass the roadworks and she did so with her nose in the air. The boy ogled her and shouted something.

Susan relaxed against her pillows. She had forgotten Louise and Bob, Paul's terrors, Julian's flippant unconcern. A much older woman crossed the road this time, but she too earned a heartening whistle. Susan smiled to herself, a little ashamed of getting amusement from something so puerile. How old did a woman have to be, she wondered, to escape this salute, thirty-five, forty, *fifty*? Certainly there was an open-hearted generosity in this lack of discrimination. Perhaps you were never too old or perhaps the old man, silent and grim while the other two acknowledged passing femininity, reserved his personal whistles for his female contemporaries.

At three the boy fetched a black kettle from the hut and began to boil it on the fire. Did they know Louise was dead? Had the news reached them somehow on the winged winds of gossip? Or had one of them come innocently to the back door on Thursday to be met by Bob's bitter staring eyes and Bob's abrupt dismissal?

The tea was made, the mugs refilled. The amount of tea they drank, they obviously preferred brewing their own to fetching it from the café two hundred yards away. No doubt it had been a blow to them when their emissary had gone to to bang on Louise's door on Wednesday and got no reply. They hadn't sent the boy that time, Susan thought, but the man in his twenties who was pulling a blue jersey over his head as he crouched by the brazier.

The trench cut halfway across the road now and, having collected the mugs, the boy stationed himself on a pile of earth, a flag in his hand, to direct what little traffic passed. He swaggered, fancying himself a policeman on crossing patrol, but presently, after only two cars had passed, the blue-jersey man beckoned him back into the hole with fierce gestures. Susan felt that she was watching a silent film that would launch soon into knockabout farce, or perhaps symbolism, where movement and facial expression are of deep significance and the human voice a vulgar intrusion.

And it was thus that Doris found her when she brought Paul home to put him to bed at six. The workmen had gone home and Susan lay back, looking dreamily at the dull crimson lights they had left behind them. She was absurdly disappointed that it was Sunday tomorrow, resentful like an avid viewer who knows he must wait two days for the next instalment of the serial.

'I've brought you a visitor,' Doris said on Sunday afternoon. 'Guess who.'

It couldn't be Julian, for he was staying in the country with Lady Maskell, part, no doubt, of a jolly gathering that would include Minta Philpott, Greg and Dian, and heaven knew who else. Besides, Julian avoided sickrooms.

'It's Bob.' Doris glanced nervously over her shoulder as his tread sounded on the stairs. 'He *would* come. I told him that in his low state he was vulnerable to every germ that's going, but he *would* come.'

His arms were full of daffodils. Susan was sure they were the ones that grew in the Braeside front garden and now she pictured that big square bed covered with the stubble of broken stalks. Louise had loved her bulbs and Bob's action in picking these flowers reminded Susan of a story she had once heard of the gardeners at Lady Jane Grey's home lopping the heads off all the oaks on the estate when she was killed. She said nothing of this to Bob. At first the sight of him embarrassed her and she wondered if he regretted his lack of reserve on Friday evening. But he showed no awkwardness, although his manner, until Doris had left them, was somewhat guarded.

'I rather expected you'd have gone away,' Susan said. 'Not exactly for a holiday, but just for a change.'

'There's nowhere I fancy going. All the places I've ever wanted to go to, I went with her.' He fetched a vase and arranged the daffodils, but clumsily for so graceful a man, crowding the stalks together and snapping them off roughly when they were too long. 'I'm better here,' he said, and when Doris thrust her head round the door with a bright smile, 'I've a lot of things to see to.'

'You're unlucky with your holidays, anyway,' Doris said. 'I remember last year Louise was ill and you were in that boat disaster.' Bob didn't say anything but his face darkened dangerously. 'Poor Louise had just what you've got now, Susan, and Bob had to amuse himself as best he could. Poor Louise said the holiday was just a dead loss as far as she was concerned. Oh dear, would you rather I didn't talk about her, Bob?'

'Please,' Bob said tightly. He sat down by Susan's bed, scarcely concealing his impatience as Doris twittered on about Paul's refusal to clean his teeth, his insistence on keeping the new watch under his pillow. 'Thank God she's gone,' he said when at last the door closed. 'Doesn't she drive you mad?'

'She's a good friend, Bob. Awfully kind.'

'She doesn't miss anything that goes on in this street. That dog of hers nearly sent me out of my mind when the funeral cars came.' He gave an unhappy sigh and suddenly Susan had for him what he had seemed to want all along, a fellow-feeling. Pity welled up in her so that, had she been well, she would have wanted to take him in her arms and hold him close to her as she might have held Paul. The thought startled her. Had it come to her because he looked so young, so pitiably vulnerable? He was older than she, four or five years older. For a moment she was embarrassed, almost dismayed.

He went to the door, opened it a fraction, then closed it softly. She thought he moved like a cat. No, like something less domestic. Like a panther. 'Got rid of those letters all right, did you?' His voice had the elaborate casual lightness of someone asking a question intensely but secretly important to him. 'That scum Heller's letters,' he said. 'You said you'd burn them.'

'Of course I did,' Susan said firmly. But the question jolted her, bringing the singing back to her head as if her temperature had swiftly taken a sharp rise. Until now she had forgotten all about the letters. They had been distasteful to her, she thought, and perhaps what had taken place in her mind was what Julian called a psychological block. Now, in spite of what she had said so reassuringly to Bob, she simply couldn't remember whether she had burnt the letters or not. Had she before, after or even during that dream-filled two hour sleep that had almost been a coma, dropped the letters into the disused fireplace and set fire to them with her lighter? Or could they possibly be still on the table, exposed for Doris or Mrs Dring to read?

'I knew I could rely on you, Susan,' Bob said. 'Sorry if I was a bore the other night.' He picked up the book she had left face-downwards. 'Highbrow stuff you read! When I'm ill I only want to lie still and look out of the window.'

'That's what I did yesterday. I just watched the workmen most of the day.'

'Fascinating pastime,' he said rather coldly, and then, 'A rotten lonely life you lead, Susan. All these months you must have been lonely and I never gave it a thought.'

'Why should you?'

'I lived next door to you. I should have realised. Louise might have realised ...' He paused and said, his voice charged with a dull anger, 'Only she was too busy with her own affairs. Or should I say affair? How old are you, Susan?'

'Twenty-six.'

'Twenty-six! And when you're under the weather you're stuck in a suburban bedroom with no one to look after you and nothing better to do than watch four or five labourers dig up the road.'

It would be useless to tell him that for a few hours that suburban bedroom had been like a theatre box and the men actors on a distant comedy stage. Bob was such a physical, down-to-earth person, a prey to strong emotions but hardly the sort of man to get pleasure from the quiet observation of human behaviour. With his looks and his extrovert attitude to life, he had probably seldom experienced the taking of a back seat. He was looking at her now with such concern that she wondered why she had ever thought him selfish. She tried to laugh but her throat was too sore.

'But I'm not alone all the time,' she said, her voice rapidly disintegrating into a croak. 'And Doris is looking after me beautifully.'

'Yes, you said she'd been a good friend. I wish you'd said it of me. I wish things had been different so you *could* have said it of me.'

There was no reply to that one. He got up abruptly and when he came back, Paul was with him, the watch still strapped round his wrist at the edge of his pyjama sleeve.

'I can't kiss you, darling. I'm all germs.'

'You haven't got a clock in here,' Paul said. 'Would you like my watch, just for tonight?'

'That's a kind thought, but I wouldn't dream of depriving you.'

His look of relief was unmistakable. 'Well, good night, then.'

'Here, let's see if I can lift you.' Bob put out his hands to clasp the boy's waist. 'You've got so tall. I bet you weigh a ton.' It gave Susan a faintly sad shock to see that hard bitter face so suddenly tender. He had no children of his own, but now . . . Of course he would marry again. Perhaps because it was too soon to have such hopes for him, the thought was vaguely displeasing.

Paul let Bob pick him up, but when the man's arms tried to swing him high as if he were a tiny child, he struggled and said babyishly, 'Put me down! Put me down!'

'Come on now, don't be silly.' Susan was tired now. She wished they would all go and leave her. Paul would take a long time getting off to sleep tonight. Let Bob think her son had protested because he didn't care to be babied; she knew that there was another darker reason.

'Good night, Susan.' The rejection hadn't upset him at all and now he gave her the charming boyish smile that made her forget how sullenly that dark face could cloud. It was such a frank, untroubled smile, ingratiating almost. She felt strangely that he had made these overtures to her son to please her rather than from a fondness for children.

'Good night, Bob. Thank you for the flowers.'

'I'll come again soon,' he said. 'Don't think you've seen the last of me.' They were alone now. He went to the door and hesitated. 'You've been my lifeline, Susan. You've been a light in the darkness.'

Less than a week ago she had been prepared to go to any lengths to avoid him. Now it seemed a cowardly, impossibly exclusive way to have behaved. Far from being selfish, he was kind, thoughtful, impulsive, all those things that Julian had never been. But she didn't know why she should compare him with Julian at all—they were so utterly different, in looks, in temperament, in manner to her—unless it was because her former husband was the only other man she could truthfully say she knew.

When the repetitive sing-song, the 'Tick-tock, tick-tock', softly chanted from Paul's bedroom ceased, Susan put on her dressing-gown, checked that her son was asleep, and made her way downstairs. Her legs were weak and each step sent a throbbing through her body up into her head.

The living-room was neater than Mrs Dring ever left it. Susan's eyes went immediately to the coffee table where she last remembered having seen Heller's letters, but there was only a clean ashtray on the polished circular expanse. She moved slowly about the room, leafing absurdly through a pile of magazines, opening drawers. This, she thought, putting her hand to her forehead, was how an underwater swimmer must feel, struggling to make a free passage through a cumbersome, unfamiliar heaviness. The air in this room seemed thick, dragging her limbs.

Doris would have loved to read those letters.

It was an unforgivable thought to have about so kind a friend. Besides, Doris would never have taken them out of the house. Susan moved aside the firescreen and peered into the grate. There was no paper ash on the clean bars.

For all that, she must have burnt them herself. And now as she cast her mind back to those dazed fever-filled hours, she could almost convince herself that she remembered holding the letters in the fireplace and watching her lighter flame eat across the pages to devour Heller's words. She could see it clearly just as she could picture Doris tidying the grate, dustpan and brush in her hand.

Her relief nearly equalled total peace of mind and if she was again shivering uncontrollably it was only because she was still ill and had disobeyed the doctor's instructions to stay in bed.

Chapter Ten

The soft insinuating voice at the other end of the line was peculiarly persistent. 'Bernard thought such a lot of you, David. He often talked about you. It seems a pity to lose touch and I know Carl wants to meet you again. We were both disappointed when you couldn't stay and have a meal on Friday, so I wondered if you'd make it another time. Say tomorrow?'

'I'm afraid I couldn't make it tomorrow.'

'Tuesday, then?'

'I can't make it this week at all. I'll ring you, shall I?' David said good-bye firmly and hung up. Then he went back into the untidy, cluttered but interesting room he called a studio and thought about it.

She had a face like Goya's *Naked Maja*, full-lipped, sensuous. It didn't attract him. He was always finding resemblances between living people and people painted long ago. Portraits were pinned all over his walls. Ganymede reproductions, picture gallery postcards, pages cut out of Sunday paper colour supplements. Vigée Le Brun's *Marie Antoinette* was there, stuck up with Sellotape next to an El Greco *Pope*; Titian's *L'homme aux Gants* had a frame which was more than he had accorded to his Van Gogh peasants or the Naked Maja herself.

A peculiar inconsistent woman, he thought, and he wasn't thinking about the Goya. She had been surly to him on the night before her husband's death and actually dismayed to see him in The Man in the Iron Mask. And then, after five minutes stilted courtesy on his part and absent-minded rejoinders on hers, she had changed her entire personality, becoming sweet, seductive and effusive. Why?

They said that no man can resist a pretty woman who throws herself at him. His nature is such that he succumbs, unable to believe such good fortune. And if he has not himself made the slightest overture, he congratulates himself, while despising the woman, on his irresistible attractions. But it hardly ever happens that way, David thought. It had never happened to him before. There had been no difficulty at all in resisting. From the first he had been bewildered.

And yet he would have done nothing about it. The incident would have been dismissed to the back of his mind, along with various others of life's apparently insoluble mysteries. People were peculiar, human nature a perennial puzzle. You had to accept it.

But she had telephoned him, talking like an old friend who had every hope and every justification for that hope of becoming much more. From a vague uneasiness, his bewilderment grew until it crowded everything else from his mind. No matter how carefully he thought about it, going over and over the events of Friday night, he could only justify Magdalene Heller's conduct by assuming her to be not quite sane. But he knew that this conclusion is always the lazy and cowardly resort of a poor imagination. Mad she might be, but there would be method in her madness. Young widows do not go into West End pubs on the day of a husband's inquests; they do not dress in tight trousers and tight sweaters; above all they do not make inexplicable unprovoked passes at casual acquaintances.

She said she had been there to meet someone and he had never for a moment believed that someone was a woman. Then he remembered the man who had come in, who had stared at her, hesitating, before retreating in haste. From that precise moment her manner towards David had changed.

Suddenly David knew quite certainly that her appointment had been with this man. She had arranged to meet a man at the pub, but the meeting must be a secret one. Why else had she failed to make the necessary introductions, denied recognising that face which now, as David remembered it, had worn in that first instant a look of satisfaction, of pleasurable anticipation? She knew him. She guessed that David's curiosity had been aroused, so she had staged the scene in the car to blind him, to seduce him and, ultimately, to make him forget what he had seen.

It must be terribly important to her, he thought, and he recalled her nervous gabbling and the urgency of her caressing hand. She had detained him in the pub after the man had gone. Because, having speculated as to the man's identity, he might have looked for him in the street, and seeing his face in daylight, have made absolute recognition certain?

But he and Hellers had, as far as he knew, no acquaintances in common. How could he have recognised a friend of Magdalene's? And, supposing he had, why did it matter so much to her?

Suddenly it had grown too warm for a fire, even outside. The roadmen had brought a spirit stove with them and the boy boiled their kettle on it inside the hut. For the first time, as if lured out by the fine weather, the man in the blue jersey was working above ground, and for the first time too, Susan saw him standing erect.

She was surprised to see that he was rather short, or, rather, short in the leg. Perhaps it was the length of his torso which had deceived her. She had a strong impression that she associated this man with height, but she didn't know why.

Then it came to her that on one previous occasion she had seen him walking along on level ground. She had seen him in Louise's garden on the day of Louise's death, and now, as she thought about it, the impression of a much taller man strengthened and grew vivid. Surely that man had been quite six feet tall and more slightly built than Blue Jersey who, swinging a pick, showed a thick waistline and a heavily muscled back.

The answer must be that at that time there had been more than three men working on the road. When he brought the daffodils, Bob had spoken of four or five men and no doubt he was better-informed on this matter than she who had scarcely spared the labourers a second glance until illness brought them into compelling perspective.

That illness was now receding and by the middle of the week Susan had lost interest in the workmen. Their doings had lost their freshness or her own standard of entertainment, lowered by fever, had risen. She read her Proust, hardly distracted even by the spasmodic scream of the drill.

'Mr North popped in with some books,' Mrs Dring piled a stack of new magazines on the bed. 'I reckon it's been the best thing that could have happened for him, you being ill. It's taken him out of himself, stopped him brooding. He coming in here again tonight, is he? You want to mind your neighbours don't get talking. That Mrs Gibbs had got a tongue as long as your arm.'

'Oh, rubbish,' Susan said crossly, 'You said yourself he only comes for something to occupy his mind.'

'And he's the type that occupies his mind with women. You needn't look like that. I dare say there's no harm in it. Men are men when all's said and done. My husband's different, but then he's one in a million as I've always said. And talking of men, if you're going to start sitting up you want to watch that lot in the road don't see you all in your nothings.'

Mrs Dring's manner was more that of a nanny than a charwoman. Susan let her draw the curtains half across the window and accepted, with a meek shrug, the bedjacket that was tossed on to the pillow.

'How many men are there working on the road, Mrs Dring?'

'Just the three.'

'I thought there were four or five last week.'

'There was never more than three,' said Mrs Dring. 'That was your temperature making you see double. There's always been just the three.'

Magdalene Heller phoned David again on Wednesday evening. She was very lonely, she said, she hardly knew a soul but Carl.

'What about your friend you were meeting in the pub?'

'I don't know him that well.'

'Better than me, surely?' Did she know what she had said? He muttered a quick good-bye. Her voice after that fatal sentence had sounded stunned. This was no fear of being caught out in a clandestine adventure, no fear of scandal. David sensed that she was deathly afraid. He had guessed right and located the source of her fear, her sudden change of heart, her advances to himself, and briefly he was elated. She wouldn't bother with him again.

Of course she had set herself up as very pure, the essence of wronged womanhood in the coroner's court. It would look funny if it turned out she had a man friend of her own, and he remembered how he had thought she was going to meet a man when he had watched her visiting the cinema. It might be a thought to read that inquest report again and see just what she had said.

Presently he unearthed the old newspaper—he always kept newspapers for weeks and weeks, finally bundling them up and putting them on top of his tiny dustbin—but the report was brief and very little of what Magdalene had said was quoted. With a shrug, he folded the newspaper again and then his eye was caught by a front-page photograph on the previous Wednesday's copy of the *Evening News*. The caption beneath it said, 'Mr Robert North and his wife Louise, who was today found shot with Bernard Heller, a 33-year-old salesman. This picture was taken while the Norths were on holiday in Devon last year. Story on page 5.'

David's eyes narrowed and he looked searchingly into the photographed face. Then he turned quickly to page five. 'I had never even heard Heller's name,' North had told the coroner, 'until someone in the street where I live told me that *Equatair*'s rep. had repeatedly called at my house. I never saw him till he was dead and I certainly didn't know he was a married man.'

But six hours later he had walked into a Soho pub where he had arranged to meet that married man's widow.

A regular weekly feature of *Certainty* was a kind of diary written entirely by Julian Townsend and called 'Happenings'. In fact, as few things ever happened to Julian and he was incurably lazy, the diary consisted less of accounts of events attended by him than a *mélange* of his opinions. There was usually some local war going on for Julian to condemn and advise negotiation or arbitration; some bill being placed before Parliament which enraged him; some politician whose way of life annoyed him and offered him an occasion of mischief-making. When, as occasionally happened, a freak silly season occurred, Julian vented his vituperation on old-established customs and institutions, spitting venom at the Royal Family, the Church of England, horse racing, musical comedies and the licensing laws.

This week 'Happenings' was as usual headed by Julian's name writ large on a streamer beneath which the writer's face scowled from a single column block. The high bumpy forehead, glossy with the sweat of intellect, round metal-framed glasses and supercilious mouth were familiar to David as a constant reader of *Certainty* and now he scarcely noticed them. A girl-friend of his, a television actress called Pamela Pearce, claimed acquaintance with *Certainty*'s editor and occasionally threatened to introduce him to David. But up till now he had steered clear of the encounter, preferring to keep his illusions. Townsend could hardly be as pompous, as self-opinionated and as pedantic as his articles led the reader to believe. David felt he might lose his zest for 'Happenings' if its writer turned out to be unassuming.

There was always a discourse on food and today Julian had gone to town, devoting the whole of his first column to recipes for aphrodisiac meat dishes and puddings, with erudite references to Norman Douglas, and half his second to a violent condemnation of the lunch he had eaten in a country hotel while week-ending with his aristocratic in-laws.

Smiling, David passed on. Apparently the fellow was going to fill up the rest of his space with an attack on the suburbs of London. 'Happenings' was a misnomer for this spate of vitriol. 'Rural England castrated by the entrenching tool, the pneumatic drill,' David read, amused. From the ravaged countryside, Julian sped towards the metropolis. 'Matchdown Park, where never a month passed without the demolition of yet another Georgian jewel . . .'

Rather odd. Years went by without a mention of Matchdown Park and now it was constantly in the news. David was surprised to find Townsend actually lived there. But he evidently did. 'The present writer's knowledge,' the paragraph ended, 'is based on five years' sojourn in the place.'

David fetched the blue S to Z telephone directory and there it was: Julian M. Townsend, 16 Orchard Drive, Matchdown Park. He hesitated, pondering. But when he began to dial, it wasn't the number on the page in front of him.

'Julian Townsend?' said Pamela Pearce. 'You're in

luck, as it happens, darling. I'm going to a party tomorrow night and he's bound to be there. Why not come along?'

'Will his wife be there?'

'His wife? I expect so. He never goes anywhere without her.'

A Mrs Susan Townsend had found Heller's body, and she lived next door to the Norths in Orchard Drive. It was all in the paper and it must be the same woman. What he would say when he met her David hardly knew, but it should be easy to bring the conversation round to the North tragedy. It would still be a hot topic with her. She had been a friend of Mrs North. Didn't the paper say she had been paying an ordinary morning call? She would know if North and Magdalene Heller had known each other before the inquest and, since she had been in court, could tell him if North's statements—'I didn't even know he was a married man' and so on—had been misreported or if, when heard in their full and proper context, were capable of a different innocent interpretation. If she were co-operative, she could set his mind at rest.

For it was active and troubled enough now. North had come to meet Magdalene in The Man in the Iron Mask six hours after the inquest. That was just explicable. He could have done so and still not have lied to the coroner. But if something else which David suspected were true, he had lied blackly and irredeemably.

They had arranged to meet there. That he knew for certain. Had they ever met there before?

Chapter Eleven

'It's a crying shame the mess them floors get in,' said Mrs Dring on all-fours. 'There's holes in this parquet you could put your finger in.' Louise's heels, Susan thought with a pang. Probably they would never be eradicated, but at least the new occupant need never know how they had been caused. Of this prospective buyer she now had high hopes, for, once well again, her first task had been to call at the estate agent's. She watched Mrs Dring obliterating small clayey footmarks, her interest caught when she said, 'Let's hope we've seen the last of all this mud. Did you know they've finished the road at last? The three of them filled up that hole of theirs last night and good riddance.'

She had seen the last act of their play, then. Settling at her typewriter, Susan wondered why they had ever dug that series of trenches and whether life in Matchdown Park would have been brought to a standstill without the monotonous rhythm of those drills and the renewing of those glimpsed cables. Her ability to concentrate and reason normally, rediscovered in the past two days, brought her intense pleasure. It seemed to her that her illness had marked the end of a black period in her life and during that illness she had found fresh resources, decided to break away from Matchdown Park and made a friend in Bob North.

But as she worked, congratulating herself on her recovery, a tiny thread of doubt crept across her mind. For some unexplored reason she was troubled by her recollections of the roadmen and although she should have shared Mrs Dring's relief at their departure, she began instead to feel a curious dismay.

There had never been more than three men, Mrs Dring insisted, and yet while Louise was lying dead with Heller she had seen a fourth man in Louise's garden. That man had knocked at Louise's back door—Mrs Dring had heard him do so—and then walked away, not to join the others, but off by himself down the road. Recapturing the scene, lifting her eyes from the type which had blurred, Susan remembered quite clearly that the three others, the old man, Blue Jersey and the boy, had been in their trench while he stood for a moment, hooded, anonymous, to warm his hands at their fire.

'Mrs Dring.' She got up, feeling a faint sickness, the

aftermath of her flu. 'I've just remembered something, something rather worrying. I suppose I was getting this flu while I was at the inquest. Only—only they asked me if I'd seen anyone call next door during the morning and I said I hadn't. I said ...' She stopped, appalled at the curiosity which almost amounted to hunger on Mrs Dring's uplifted face.

'Well, you didn't see no one, did you?'

'I'd forgotten. It can't matter now. We all knew what the verdict was going to be, but still ...' And Susan bit her lip, not because of what she had said, but because she had said it to this woman, this bearer of malice, this arch troublemaker who had no kind word for anyone but her husband. Then she managed a strained smile and, convincing herself she was changing the subject, said, 'You'll have a chance to get the floors nice now Paul won't be bringing in any more clay on his shoes.'

Gin and the 'something fizzy' he always liked to drink with it, coffee cups on a tray, the last of the daffodils displayed in a vase. Susan had only made these preparations once before but already they were becoming a ritual. Bob would be late tonight—he couldn't be with her until ten, for he had a business call to make—but she had already given up going to bed early. There was something to stay up for.

'It's always so wonderfully warm in here, Susan,' he said as he entered the living-room. 'There's a lot to be said for central heating. I don't know why I didn't have it put in years ago.'

She turned her head away to hide the blush, but, although she was aware of his solecism, she felt a rush of elation. In saying such a thing, he had showed her that while Louise's death was fresh in his mind, the circumstances which had led up to it were fading. Would it be right to trouble him now with the question she had been intending to put to him all day? In all their talks they had scarcely yet discussed any subject but that of Heller and Louise, and just the same she hesitated, waiting for him to begin as he always did, obsessively, minutely on the details of their love and death.

A lightness and a sense of relief came to her when instead he asked her casually if she knew of anyone who would do the Braeside housework for him.

'My Mrs Dring might. I'll ask her.'

'You've done so much for me, Susan, and here I am still asking favours.'

'A very small favour. She may not be able to.'

'Somehow I feel she will if you ask her. You're one of those people who make things come right. D'you know, in the past week I've often thought that if we'd really bothered to get to know you, if you and Louise had been friends, none of this would ever have happened.'

They were back to it again. Subject normal.

'If I'm really so powerful,' Susan said, an urgency entering her voice, 'If I can really make things come right, I'd like to begin by telling you to stop all that, Bob. Try to forget it, put it behind you.'

He reached out and took her hands, both her hands in a strong warm grasp. For a comforter, a safe refuge, she suddenly felt strangely weak and enervated.

Pamela Pearce was a pretty little blonde with a taste for glitter. Metallic threads ran through the materials of most of her clothes; she liked sequins and beads and studs, anything that sparkled. Tonight she wore lamé, and against the cobbles and the grey brick walls of the South Kensington mews she glittered like a goldfish in murky waters.

'Hadn't you better tell me who my host and hostess are?' David said as he locked his car. 'I don't want to feel like a complete gatecrasher.'

'Greg's one of those society photographers. You must have seen those lovely things he did of Princess Alexandra. His wife's called Dian and she's absolutely lovely. You'll fall madly in love with her. Believe me, just to see her is to adore her.'

The trouble was David was never quite sure whether

he had seen her. He was hardly in a position to fall madly in love with her as nobody bothered to introduce him to anyone and, Pamela having been borne off up the narrow staircase, he found himself alone on an island of carpet, surrounded by indifferent backs. Presently he forced his way between barathea-jacketed backs and half-naked backs, moving his arms like a swimmer doing the breast stroke, and finally squeezing into a little lyre-backed chair. A screen behind him was perilously loaded with lighted candles which dripped wax on to an improvised bar.

For some minutes no one took any notice of him and Pamela didn't reappear. Then a voice behind him said incomprehensibly, 'Do you think you could get outside some cup?'

David looked over his shoulder, first at the young man with butter-coloured hair who had addressed him, then at the bar where in a bowlful of pale golden liquid cherries and pieces of cucumber were floating. Before he could say he would avoid this at any price, a ladleful had been scooped up and dribbled into a glass.

It tasted like fruit juice which someone had poured into a cough mixture bottle. David put his glass down behind a plate of smoked eel canapes, observing that everyone else seemed also to have shunned the cup.

The room was too small to accommodate so large a party, but even so the guests had succeeded in huddling themselves into distinctly isolated groups. The largest of these had for its nucleus a tall man with an enormous forehead and he stood beneath the central lamp which effectively spotlighted him. David had no difficulty in recognising Julian Townsend.

The editor's prim mouth was opening and shutting nineteen to the dozen while he gesticulated sweepingly with a large hand in which he held a sausage roll. Five women stood around him in a circle, hanging on his words.

One of them must be his wife, David thought, the innocent neighbor of Heller's mistress, she who had found the dead couple. There was a statuesque brunette with a cigar, two nearly identical blondes, a teen-ager in brown and an elderly lady who evidently intended to spend the rest of the weekend in the country, for she wore a tweed suit, mesh stockings and tall boots. Pamela was nowhere to be seen, although he could hear her shrill giggle occasionally from upstairs, and he felt a stab of annoyance. Short of introducing himself as a reader and a fan, he couldn't see how he was going to talk to Townsend without her.

Then the teen-ager detached herself from the sycophantic circle and made for the bar. Her movements had the rapid and entirely selfish directness of the very young and, to avoid her, David backed into the bamboo screen.

'Good gracious, you nearly set your hair on fire!' The butter-haired barman had seized his arm and David backed away from the naked candle-flame.

'Thanks,' he said, his face inches from the girl's.

'You need someone to look after you, don't you?' said the barman. 'It quite upsets me to see you standing there all lost. Take him under your wing, Elizabeth, do.'

Having refused the cup and helped herself to brandy, the girl said baldly, 'I'm Elizabeth Townsend. What's your name?'

'David Chadwick.' He was very surprised and perhaps he showed it. In her very short shapeless dress of the colour and texture of brown bread and with her long untidy brown hair she looked about seventeen. No doubt accustomed to being in the company of a man never at a loss for words, she fixed him with an incredulous glare. 'I believe you live in Matchdown Park,' he heard himself say in exactly the tone of wistful awe someone might use when enquiring if an acquaintance had a grace and favour apartment at Hampton Court.

'My God, no. Whatever gave you that idea?'

'I read it in *Certainty*,' David said indignantly. 'You *are* Mrs Julian Townsend?'

'Of course I am.' She looked deeply affronted. Then her brow, furrowed with impatience and some imagined slight, cleared. 'Oh, I see it all now. You've dropped a clanger.' His discomfiture stirred a gurgle from the depths of the brown bread dress. 'That's his ex you're thinking of, my—well, what would you call her?—wife-in-law might fit, don't you think?' She giggled happily at her own joke. 'Wild horses wouldn't make me live in Matchdown Park.' She said this with violent defiance, but almost before the words were out something quick and sharp came into her expression to change it and make it assume a slight concupiscence. 'Why d'you ask, anyway? Have you got some sort of yen to live in the place?'

'I might,' David muttered, not knowing where all this was leading. Never in all his life had he met anyone so brutally direct and unselfconscious as this girl. He wondered on what her confidence was built, plain, dumpy and charmless as she was.

'Only my wife-in-law . . .' She grinned with delight at her invented expression. '. . . my wife-in-law wants to move, so Julian's got this house in Matchdown Park on his hands. It's a very good sort of house.' She seemed sublimely unconscious that two minutes before she had denounced its environs with a shudder. 'Julian would be absolutely ecstatic if I'd found a buyer for him.'

Next door to Norths, inhabited by the woman who knew the Norths, who had found Heller's body. The candles flared behind David's head and their reflections, tall, smoky, yellow-white, danced in Elizabeth Townsend's glass. 'How big is it?' he said cautiously.

'Come and meet Julian. He'll tell you all about it.' She grabbed his arm, her fingers, urgent and almost affectionate, digging into his elbow. 'Julian, do shut up a minute! Listen, I've found a bloke who actually wants to live in Matchdown Park!'

Susan hadn't warned Paul that Bob was coming in for the evening. She didn't want him to awaken and, troubled by fears and fantasies as he was, hear a man's voice downstairs. In his present world men who called on solitary women brought guns with them . . .

Murmuring an excuse to Bob, she went up to Paul's bedroom, tucked him in again, restored his watch to a more secure position on the bedside table and went out again, leaving the light burning. She was half-way down the stairs when the phone rang.

'I don't suppose you've sold the house yet?' Julian's voice sounded unnaturally enthusiastic against a background of music and hilarity.

'Hardly,' Susan said dryly.

'That's what I thought. However, not to worry. Now tell me, are you doing anything on Monday night?'

She no longer loved him but it was horrible to be asked such a question by the man who had once been her husband.

'Why?'

'I've told some fellow he can come and look over the house. Chadwell, Challis—something like that. He's here with me now as a matter of fact—well, not exactly with me but we're all at Dian's and Elizabeth picked him up.'

'I thought you must be. I can hardly hear you for the racket. How is Dian?'

'Absolutely lovely as usual.'

Susan cleared her throat. 'What time does this man want to come?'

'Eightish. By the by . . .' He lowered his voice to a barely audible mumble. 'I shouldn't mention that peculiar affair next door. It might put him off.'

'Julian, you must be more naïve than I think you if you imagine anyone could go through all the fuss of buying this house without finding out about Louise's suicide.' She stopped, aghast. All the doors were open and Bob must have heard. Too late now. 'Oh, Julian!' she said, exasperated.

'He might not find out,' Julian said craftily, 'until he'd signed the contract. Don't tell me you're indifferent to the prospect of five thousand pounds. Now I must return to this do. I suppose you're all alone?'

'In point of fact,' Susan said, 'I'm not. A friend is with me, so if you'll excuse me, Julian, I'd better get back to him.'

Bob sat where she had left him, on his face the blank look of someone who has been unable to help overhearing a private conversation but who must pretend, from politeness, to a temporary total deafness.

'Sorry about that,' Susan said crisply. 'You must have heard.'

'I couldn't help it. I gather you're thinking of moving, Susan?'

'The atmosphere here isn't right for Paul, and besides that ... I suppose I wasn't well, I was almost hysterical at the end of last week. I wanted to get away as soon as possible, but that was before ...'

Before what? What had she been about to say? Confused, she turned her head away. She had waited for him to finish the sentence for her and instead his glance was cool, analytical, assessing.

'When d'you think you'll go?'

'As soon as I can,' she said evenly, and then she made herself smile, crushing down the absurd disappointment. Had she really supposed this widower, this lost soul almost, came to see her because he was growing fond of her? He wanted a shoulder to cry on merely, and hers was waiting.

'I can understand you want to shake the dust of this place off your feet,' he said, 'put all the misery behind you. You'll soon forget about Louise and me, won't you?' Then, obsessively, forgetting perhaps that he had said it all before a dozen times, he began step by step to go over every word, action and suspicion that had led him to suspect Louise's love affair, to search again into the circumstances of her death.

'Bob,' Susan said sharply, 'you'll have to stop this. You'll turn yourself into a neurotic. What do you hope to gain by it? They're both dead, it's all over.' He looked at her, shocked and silenced. For the first time she was asking herself why, when another man would put up an outward show of courage, he should be so obsessed by his wife's death. A little thrill of nervousness, not quite fear, at the enormity of what she was about to say, ran through her. 'It isn't because . . .' she began slowly, 'it isn't because you doubt that it *was* suicide, is it?'

He made no answer. His smoky blue eyes had a glazed look and his face went dead so that the lamplight seemed to fall on a copper mask.

Susan's own words had startled her and now that they were out she was sure they would have been better unsaid. She had no grounds at all for saying them, only a vague unease that during the day and the previous day had held her standing sometimes in a dream or sent her upstairs to stare meaninglessly out of the window.

'It's just that, while I was ill . . .' She blushed hotly. Was this how Doris felt when she made one of her gaffes? 'There were one or two things,' she said, 'one or two odd things that made me wonder.'

'You were delirious.'

'Come now, I wasn't that ill.'

'I shouldn't want,' he said, 'I couldn't bear . . . Susan, it was his gun, they found the powder marks on his hand. How could there be . . . ?'

'If you don't think so,' she said, 'of course there can't be any doubt.' And she felt cold and sick because he was on his feet now. She had been his comforter and now he must think her just like all the others, stirring up trouble for him, making use of him as a topic for speculation. Wordlessly, he had moved out into the hall to stand on the spot where Louise's heel had pierced the parquet.

'Bob,' she said, going to him.

'Susan?'

'I was delirious.'

He touched her shoulder, bent down and brushed her cheek with his lips. It seemed like ages since anyone but Paul had kissed her and as she felt the light touch of his mouth she fancied she could still hear quite clearly the laughter and the music from that party far away, as if the telephone was still open, still transmitting it. A loneliness that was abysmal and a desire to end that loneliness at all costs, made her put out her hand and take his, holding it tightly.

'Forgive me?'

He nodded, still too shaken to smile. She heard him walk swiftly into Braeside but although, after a sick empty interval, she too went out into the garden, she saw that no lights had come on in the house next door where the windows were always closed.

Chapter Twelve

The trees which grew from rectangles in the pavement were the kind David most disliked, sterile ornamental cherries and prunuses which bear no fruit. They were in full blossom now and he guessed that he had picked for his visit the one day in the year on which Orchard Drive justified its name. The buds had all opened, not a petal had yet fallen, and the flowers reminded him of crêpe paper. Behind the pink cloudy masses street lamps glowed with the acid drop quality of milky quartz.

He drove along slowly, following the route Heller had taken to see his love. The houses would only appear large to those with small horizons. They were not all the same—he counted four different types—but each was detached, each had an integral garage and a biggish lawned or landscaped front garden. He passed doors painted lilac and doors painted lime; he noted here the pretentious bay tree and there the pair of mass-produced carriage lamps. No raised voice, no subdued strain of music, no footfall disturbed the silence. He was beginning to see why wild horses wouldn't have dragged Elizabeth Townsend to live here.

Rather like a wild horse herself or perhaps a shaggy

Shetland pony, she had tugged him toward the group where the editor of *Certainty* was holding forth. With a shout of 'Do me a favour, Minta,' and 'Mind your backs!' she had shoved him unceremoniously under her husband's nose.

Julian Townsend raised his eyebrows and one deprecating hand in his wife's direction. ' . . . And just that essential dash of cointreau,' he finished. 'It makes all the difference between common *potage* and *haute cuisine*. Now, what was it you wanted to say, my darling?'

The female sycophants edged away. David looked awkwardly into the face that each week launched a thousand outraged letters. A faint dew glistened on Townsend's bulbous forehead and it creased and smoothed again as his little brown wife introduced David inaccurately.

'A private transaction would be nice, of course,' the great man said at last. 'Not that I'd consider less than ten thousand.'

'Not exorbitant these days.'

This casual rejoinder threw Townsend slightly off balance. It was apparent that he was thinking quickly, perhaps dismayed that he had named so paltry a sum. But, the mobile supercilious face having worked for some seconds, he seemed to abandon that line to say almost meekly. 'It's a delightful area, *rus in urbe*, you know. The house itself is in excellent condition. Do you know the district well?'

David, who had occasionally passed through it on the tube and heard it twice mentioned by Bernard Heller, said that he did. Townsend beamed at him.

'I really do think this calls for a drink.' He made no move to fetch drinks himself, but a kind of telepathy seemed to pass between him and the woman called Minta. She trotted off and returned with a trayful of whiskies. Townsend raised his glass and shouted something which sounded like '*Terveydeksenne!*'

'A Finnish toast,' said Minta reverently.

So Townsend had gone off to find Dian and get her permission to use her phone. 'I do hope you buy it,' said his wife, tucking her arm into David's. 'We could do with our half-share in the ten thou. Give my love to poor old Susan.'

Well, he would see poor old Susan in a minute. This was the place next door to Braeside, innocent, respectable-looking Braeside where Heller had found something the green-eyed Magdalene could not give him and into which he had taken death.

Or had death come to him?

That, David thought, was presumably why he was here. To try to find out. To disturb this all-enveloping, blanket-like silence. The pale, dry papery flowers brushed his face as he got out of the car. He slammed the door and from behind him out of the dark stillness came an appalling frenzied roar. He jumped, wheeled round. But it was only a dog, a great ginger and black curly coated thing with a monstrous horror-film shadow that cavorted wildly in an opposite garden. David noted that a sturdy iron gate separated it from him. That was that. The noise put paid to all thoughts, very tempting natural thoughts, of giving up and returning the way he had come. Poor old Susan would have been alerted by now, was probably eyeing him from between those drawn curtains.

He marched up the drive, suddenly dreading the encounter. Would she be a facsimile of Elizabeth, strident and indiscreet, or a taboo-ridden housewife from whose genteelisms Townsend had thankfully escaped? The dog's fury pursued him embarrassingly. He rang the bell. The fact that it rang instead of evoking a carillon of Westminster chimes slightly cheered him. The hall light came on, the door opened and he stood face to face with the woman who had found Heller dead.

She was not what he had expected. Taking in the fair hair, the broad brow and the slender tilted nose, he knew at once where he had seen that face before. In the National Gallery, but not on a living woman. Effie Ruskin, he thought, Millais, *The Order of Release*. She smiled at him in a businesslike way.

'I'm sorry about the dog,' she said. 'Deafening, isn't it? He always barks like that at strangers.'

'Only at strangers?'

'Oh, yes. You needn't worry that he'll bark at you if you come to live here. Won't you come in? I'm afraid it's rather late for you to see the garden.'

A sudden dismay seized him. Pulling a fast one over Julian Townsend and his current wife was all very well. Shallow, unscrupulous, insincere, they had seemed to ask for it. This woman, who received him in good faith, impressed him at first sight as utterly honest. He sensed an old-fashioned integrity about her and it made him feel like a spy. For the past few days he had been living in a spy story world where the unconventional and the 'not done' thing was suspended. She brought him up against the hard brick wall of reality with a jolt.

Following her inside and watching her meet her own reflection, tall, shapely stylish, in the long wall glass, he thought of her supplanter and his opinion of Julian Townsend sank still further. Very probably he would give up taking *Certainty*.

'This is the living-room,' she said, 'with a dining area, you see, and that door leads to the room my—Julian, that is—used to have for his study. I'll show you in a moment.'

There was something that looked like a manuscript—perhaps she wrote—on a desk, a full ashtray beside it—she smoked too much—and on the sofa arm a copy of *Within a Budding Grove*. She had a mind too. For a prospective buyer, he was looking at all the wrong things. It was not she that was for sale.

'I'm sure you won't mind if I ask you to keep fairly quiet when we go upstairs. My little boy is asleep.'

'I didn't know you had a child.'

'Why should you?' Her cool voice chilled. She began to instruct him in the controls of the central heating plant and he thought of Heller. On the sideboard he could see a tray with a gin bottle on it, a can of some fizzy mineral water, two glasses. She was expecting someone, a man probably. Two women alone together would drink coffee or tea or perhaps sherry.

Presently she led the way upstairs. The child slept in a lighted room and he liked the way she approached the bed, tenderly and gently, to rearrange the tumbled bedclothes, but he was less happy about her troubled frown and for the first time he noticed a gauntness in her face.

Nobody slept in the main bedroom now. Bachelor though he was, he could tell an unused bed and detect that nothing lay between mattress and counterpane. She must have moved out when Townsend left her. Damn Townsend! It gave him a very real pleasure to envisage the man's disappointment when the expected 'five thou' wasn't forthcoming. For two pins he'd keep him hanging on while he, David, ostensibly made up his mind. He could take weeks about it, months. Only there was this girl. As she talked and pointed out the amenities of the place, he began to feel sick. He was practising on her a monstrous deceit, all the more reprehensible because she probably needed the sale.

She closed the bedroom door and said quietly, 'There's something I think you ought to know before we go any further. I don't know if you like the house, but I couldn't let you make an offer without telling you there was a double suicide next door. Only three weeks ago. It was in all the papers but perhaps you haven't connected it.'

Her honesty, in contrast to his deceit, brought the colour into his face. 'I did . . .'

'It wouldn't be fair not to tell you. Some people might feel superstitious about it. Mrs North and the man—a man called Heller—shot themselves in her bedroom. *This* bedroom. The houses are just the same inside.' She shrugged. 'Well, now you know,' she said.

He walked away from her and rested his hands on the banister rail. 'I did know,' he said, and in a rush, 'I knew Bernard Heller. I knew him quite well.'

The silence behind him was thick and almost

frightening. Then he heard her say, 'I don't quite understand. You knew and yet you wanted . . .'

He began to go downstairs, all his natural diffidence depriving him of words. She came slowly after him. Without looking back, he felt a quite disproportionate sorrow that the tentative friendly harmony established between them had been destroyed.

At the foot of the stairs she stood a little distance from him. 'You want to buy a house next door to the one your friend died in? I really don't understand.'

'I know Mrs Heller too and I'll try to explain . . .'

She looked towards the front door, back at him. 'It's hardly my business, but it is my business to know if you want to buy this house or not. If you're a journalist or a private detective, you ought to be next door, not here.'

'Mrs Townsend . . .'

Her eyes opened wide—grey eyes, unbearably clear—and the Effie Ruskin mouth curled as it curled in the painting. 'What exactly *did* you think? That I'd gossip, give you revelations? I don't know anything about Mrs Heller, I only saw her once, but hasn't Mr North had enough?'

She glanced up upstairs, then trying to move casually, edged past him. She was frightened. It had never occurred to him that she might be frightened, for he had never before put himself into the shoes of a lonely woman who finds herself closeted with a strange man, an impostor. He felt his face go white with shame as he watched her eye the telephone, that lifeline, that communication with protection, and he moved away, his heart pounding.

In her eyes he was the salesman who wedges his foot in the door, the soft-spoken mechanic turned rapist, the insurance collector with warped desires, latent sadism. Her hand creeping towards the receiver, she said bravely, 'Mr North is a friend of *mine*. I don't understand what you're doing, only that he isn't going to be hurt any more. Tell Mrs Heller that.'

He opened the front door. The pink crêpe paper

blossom covered the street light like a lampshade. He stepped out into the porch and once again the dog began to roar. She must know now that she was safe. 'Perhaps Mrs Heller has already told him,' he said loudly above the din.

'She has never spoken to him.' Abandoning the telephone, she lifted her head high. 'Now will you please go?'

'O God,' he said, stammering a little, cursing the dog, 'I won't hurt you. I'm going and you can phone the police if you like. I expect I've done something against the law, false pretences probably.' He couldn't meet her eyes, but he had to say it. 'Mrs Townsend, they do know each other. On the very day of the inquest they planned a meeting in a London pub. I saw them.'

The door slammed in his face, so near to his face that he had to jerk backwards quickly. The dog was so incensed by now that its antics made the gate rattle and clang. He got into his car, his hands actually shaking.

As he moved off another car passed him and swung smoothly into the Braeside drive. Only someone who did that manoeuvre every day could perform it with such practised ease. David slowed. The man got out and David saw his head in his driving mirror, a dark head, neat, perfect, a gleaming, almost metallic coin relief in the pinkish-white lamp glow. Robert North. He had only seen that face in the flesh once before.

David braked and sat still. Without turning his head, he continued to observe North in the mirror. The other man was raising his garage door now, approaching his car, changing his mind. David wondered why the silence seemed wrong somehow and then he realised that the dog had ceased to bark. No one had taken it into the house. Its long monstrous shadow, magnified into a Hound of the Baskervilles, wriggled fawningly between the shadowed bars of the gate as North approached it and patted its head. The big black silhouettes quivered. North turned away and still the dog was silent. Susan Townsend had said it only barked at strangers. . . .

North's shadow moved across the road. It was much larger and more sinister than the man who cast it. David watched him go up to Mrs Townsend's front door and ring the bell.

They were on close terms those two, he thought as he drove away. The gin and the can of fizzy stuff were for him. No wonder the girl had reacted as she had! She was not merely a good discreet neighbour; she was emotionally involved with him. Why not use old-fashioned, more realistic terms? She was in love with him. On his looks alone, he was a man any woman might love. And he, David, had thought he could sound her about North's behaviour, North's attitude.

He must have been mad to suppose he could enter into a conspiracy with a strange woman, even if that woman had not been in love, enter with her into a plot to bring about North's downfall. This was not one of those serials for which he designed sets, but the real unromantic world. Had he really supposed that at a word from him she would break the barriers of convention and loyalty and confer with him as to her friend's actions and motives?

It seemed that he had. He had genuinely believed in the possibility of setting up with Mrs Townsend a kind of amateur detective bureau and, without prior contact, they were to have banded together in a scheme to overthrow two lives.

Bob put his arm gently around her shoulders and led her to a chair. 'What's happened, Susan? You look as if you've had a shock.'

'Someone was here,' she said, breathing quickly. A man . . . He said—insinuated, if you like—that you'd met Mrs Heller secretly on the day of the inquest.'

'So I did,' he said coolly. 'I met her in a London pub, but there was nothing secret about it.'

'You don't have to tell me.' Susan moved slightly to free herself from his encircling arm. 'It isn't my business, only I thought you didn't know her. I had the impression you'd never met till the inquest.'

'We hadn't. But afterwards I talked to her—she apologised to me, as a matter of fact, for the way she'd behaved in court. I was sorry for her. She's almost destitute, you know. That swine Heller hadn't left her a penny to live on. I felt I was bound to help and that's why we met. However, when we got there I found her with a man.'

'This Chadwick who came here?'

'Yes. Susan, the last thing I felt like was talking to strangers. I'm afraid I just bolted and then I came to see you. Of course, I've seen Mrs Heller since at her home. I've just come from there now.'

'How cruel people are,' she said wonderingly.

'Some are. And then you find someone who's sweet and good and lovely like you, Susan.'

She looked up at him incredulously.

'I meant that,' he said softly. 'Come here, Susan. You lived next door to me for years and years and I never saw you. And now, I suppose it's too late ... I wonder ... Would you kiss me, Susan?'

He would touch her forehead, brush her cheek, as he had done the other day at the door. She lifted her face passively and then, suddenly, it was not like the other day at all. She was in his arms, clinging to him, mouth to mouth and eyes closing at last on their loneliness and their shared rejection.

Chapter Thirteen

Detective Inesepector Ulph knew that Robert North had killed his wife and his wife's lover. He knew it, not as he knew he was James Ulph, forty-eight years old, divorced, childless, but he knew it as a juror must, beyond a reasonable doubt.

There was nothing he could do about it. His superintendent laughed at him when he talked of North's motive and North's opportunity. Motive and opportunity cut no ice, unless it can be proved the man was there, the gun to which he had access, in his hand.

'Ever heard of a small point,' said the superintendent scathingly, 'of tracing the weapon from its source to the killer?'

Ulph had. It had perplexed him all along. Half-way through his interrogation of North he had met the man's eyes and read in them, under the simulated grief, a defiance which seemed to say, You know and I know it. It can never be proved. And as in a match there comes a point where one of the contestants knows the other will win—will win, at any rate, this hand or this game—Ulph knew that North held the good cards, that he had stacked them subtly long beforehand.

The gun was Heller's. Both Heller's widow and Heller's brother swore that it was in his possession the night before the killing. Except by unimaginable feats of burglary, by breaking into a flat of whose very existence North was certainly ignorant, he could not have gained possession of that gun. After the deaths Ulph had tested Heller's hand for powder burns and then, as if it were an embarrassing formality, North's hand also. Heller had fired shots, North none. Heller had been seen to enter Braeside at ten minutes past nine by a Mrs Gibbs and a Mrs Winter and during the rest of the morning no one had left the house. North, carless as he was once every four weeks, had been in Barnet.

And yet Ulph knew that he had killed his wife. The picture, as in a peculiarly vivid and impressive film sequence, of how he had done it first came to him during the actual process of the inquest and since then it had returned often with the insistence of a recurring dream.

No one had seen North leave his house that morning, but this, this negative thing, this not seeing, not noticing, was pathetic, laughable, when it came to a question of proof and circumstantial evidence. 'I didn't see him leave,' Mrs Gibbs had said, 'but I often don't see him leave. Not seeing someone's no help really, is it? I saw Heller come.'

Because the dog had barked ... North knew that, of course, that no one in Orchard Drive ever saw anything unless the dog barked. Ulph's dream picture unfolded at this point, or just before this point. North had shot his wife while she was making the bed and then, when the dog barked, he had gone downstairs to admit the lover.

Ulph had only seen the man dead, but again and again he saw how that heavy earnest face must have looked when the door was opened, not by his mistress but by her husband. North would have stood well behind the door so that his neighbours, watching, saw only the door itself sliding inwards. And who would have questioned this secretive and surreptitious method of admitting Heller, this action so typical of a woman conducting a clandestine adventure?

Then, after the first shock, the adrenalin rushing into Heller's bloodstream, came the quick gathering of his forces. The cover story, the subterfuge ... But North would have forestalled him, saying mildly that he was becoming genuinely interested in this idea of a heating installation. He had stayed at home to discuss it. And Heller, concealing his dismay, had followed him upstairs, entering as best he could, into his unlooked-for, fantastic conversation about radiators.

Ulph saw the dead woman lying on the bed and heard North's cry of alarm. His wife must have fainted. What more natural than for Heller to join him at the bedside, bend over—with a very real concern—the body of Louise North.

North had shot him then, shot him through the head. Had he been wearing rubber gloves? Had he perhaps come to the door with those gloves on and a teacloth in his hands? Ulph pictured those gloved hands closing the dead man's bare hand around the gun, aiming it at the dead woman's heart, pressing the trigger for the third time.

The picture stopped there, as if the projector had suddenly broken down.

North must have left the house. It was inconceivable that he could have done so and no one see him. All eyes had been on Braeside, regardless of the dog, waiting for Heller to come out. But North hadn't come out. He had come *in* at one-fifteen in his newly serviced car.

And the gun? Sometimes Ulph played fantastically with the idea that North might have taken it from him, out of his briefcase, while it stood on the kitchen table. But Heller never took that gun out of his flat. He would only have brought it with him to commit suicide. . . .

That part of Ulph which was a policeman wanted North brought to justice; that part which was an ordinary man had for him a sneaking fellow-feeling. His own wife had left him for another man and he had divorced her, but there had been times when another fantasy had occupied his mind, a fantasy not unlike that in which he saw North playing the vital role. He knew what it was like to want to kill.

That North's actions showed a long and careful premeditation did not, in Ulph's estimation, make the killing any less of a crime of passion. North had been cool, he thought, with the coolness that is a thin veneer lying on humiliated burning rage, unbearable jealousy. And the grief he had at first believed simulated might in fact be real, the horror of an Othello, who unlike Othello, had real and undeniable grounds for his crime.

So Ulph felt no desire to act as the instrument of society's revenge on North. His interest was academic, detached. He simply wanted to know how the man had done it, to a lesser extent why, when in this case divorce was the easy and obvious solution, the man had done it.

But the whole matter was closed. The coroner and the superintendent between them had closed it.

Afterwards David wished he hadn't telephoned her to apologise. Her voice still stung in his ears.

'Mr North has arranged to lend her some money. It's a pity some of her friends of longer standing didn't think of that.'

She had crushed him with cool pointed sentences, calculated to wound. But as he listened to her meekly, he could only think of the first impression she had made on him, an impression of utter sincerity. He bore her no ill-will. Unable to forget her face, he went into the Tate Gallery after work, found *The Order of Release* and then bought a postcard copy. He had made no mistake in likening her to Effie Ruskin, but now as he made his way out on to the Embankment and hailed a taxi, he found that the card which he still held in his hand brought him no pleasure, nor any satisfaction at the accuracy of his visual memory. He had the feeling that to pin it on his wall with the others might curiously depress him.

When he got to The Man in the Iron Mask the two bearded men were the only customers and they sat at their usual table, drinking shorts.

'Covenanting's all very well, Sid,' David heard Charles say, 'for the other fellow, the one who benefits, but it's a mug's game for number one.'

'Quite,' said Sid.

'What's in it for you, I mean? Sweet Fanny Adams, unless you get a kick out of doing the Inland Revenue in the eye.'

The barman eyed David curiously as, with an anxious frown, he pretended to scan the empty room.

'You look as if you've lost something.'

'Someone,' David corrected him. 'A young lady.' The genteelism grated rather. 'I hoped to find her here.'

'Stood you up, has she?'

'Not exactly.' Sid and Charles weren't going to bite. Why should they? It wasn't going to be as easy as all that. He edged diffidently towards their table. 'Excuse me.' Charles gave him an indignant glare. David thought it a bad-tempered face. 'Excuse me, but have you been in here since they opened?'

'We have.' Charles seemed about to add So what? or did David want to make something of it?

'I wondered if you'd happened to see a girl come in, striking-looking dark girl. You saw me in here with her a couple of weeks back.'

'Rings a bell.' Charles's surly expression softened and he began to look less like Rasputin. 'Wait a minute. Dishy-looking piece in tight pants, would it be?'

'Come now, Charles,' said Sid.

'No offence meant, old man. Intended as a compliment actually.'

'That's all right.' David managed a quite easy, natural laugh. 'She used to be my secretary and now my present girl's leaving me, I thought . . . The fact is I believe she's often in here and as I don't know where she's living, I came in on the off-chance of catching her.' He marvelled at his own ability to lie glibly. 'You know how it is,' he said.

'She's not been in tonight,' said Charles. 'Sorry we can't help you. I wish I'd had the nous,' he said to Sid, 'to buy a hundred Amalgamated Asphalts last week. They touched thirty-eight and six this morning.'

'Quite.'

'Can I get you a drink?' David asked desperately.

'You could have knocked me down with a feather. Six months they've been stuck at twenty-five bob and . . . Did I hear someone say the magic word drink? That's very nice of you, old man.'

'Brandy,' said Sid, apparently for both of them.

David bought two brandies and a beer for himself. The barman tightened his lips. His expression was meaningful but David couldn't interpret that meaning.

'Her boy-friend would do,' he said as he put the glasses down. 'All I want is her address.'

'*Salud y pesetas,*' said Charles 'Not that I'd say much for the peseta at this moment. You still worrying about that girl, old man?'

Casting aside caution, David said, 'Have you ever seen her in here with a man?'

Charles gave Sid a lugubrious wink. 'Time and time again. Tall, good-looking dark bloke. Always drank gin with something fizzy in it, didn't he, Sid?'

'Quite,' said Sid.

Excitement caught at David's throat, making him stammer. That Sid and Charles obviously thought him Magdalene Heller's cast-off lover didn't bother him at all. 'Always?' he said. 'You mean they've been in here often?'

'About once a week for the past six months. No, I'm wrong there. More like eight months. You can put me right on that, Sid. When did we give up The Rose and start coming here?'

'August.'

'August it was. I remember it was August because the first day I got back from Majorca Sid and I went as usual to The Rose and, damn it, if they didn't short-change me. I've had about as much of this as I can stand, I said to Sid, and so we came here instead. Your girl and the dark bloke were here then.'

'I see. And they've been meeting regularly here ever since?'

'Not for the past fornight.' Charles glanced in the barman's direction and then leant towards David confidingly. 'It's my belief they got fed up with this place. There's a lot of skulduggery goes on. Just before you came in that fellow tried to pull a fast one on me. Said I'd given him a pound when it was a fiver. Disgusting!' His brows drew together angrily and he rubbed his beard.

'It looks as if I'll have to advertise for a secretary after all.'

Sid glared at him derisively and, getting up suddenly, spoke the longest sentence David had ever heard him utter. 'Don't give me that, that secretary stuff, d'you mind? We're all men of the world, I hope, and personally I don't care to be talked down to like a school

kid. You don't want another drink, do you, Charles?'
He swung the door open. 'Secretary!' he said.

'Quite,' said Charles, reversing roles. They went.

David turned towards the bar and shrugged.

'Couple of comedians they are,' said the barman energetically. 'If you like your humour sick.'

Keyed up and tremendously elated by his discovery, David had felt he couldn't stand the pub a moment longer. He was filled with an urgent energy, and wasting it on chit-chat with the barman made him impatient. Nor did he we want to drink any more, for drink might cloud his thought processes. He went out into the street and began to walk about aimlessly.

His excitement lasted about ten minutes. While it lasted he felt as he had done at other high spots in his life, when he had got his diploma, for instance, when he had landed his present job. There was no room for anything else in his mind but self-congratulation. Heller was temporarily forgotten in a pride and an elation that had nothing to do with morality or justice or indignation. He had found it out, done what he had set out to do and now he could only reflect with wonder on his achievement.

But he was not naturally vain and by the time he came, by a circuitous route, to Soho Square his swagger was less confident. It might have been someone he had passed that recalled her to his mind, a girl with straight fair hair like hers or one whose grey eyes met his for a moment. Her image entered his mind with startling clarity and suddenly he came down to earth with a bump. He sat down on one of the seats under the trees and as his hand touched the cold metal arm a shiver ran through him.

She ought to be told. She ought not to be left there alone with no one to protect her, a prey to North. It seemed absurd to equate her with the classic detective story victim who, knowing too much, must be silenced, but wasn't that in fact what she had become? Already she had alerted North, informing him of David's early suspicions. There was no knowing how much else she had seen, living next door to North as she did, what tiny discrepancies she had observed in his behaviour. David didn't for a moment believe North sought her company from honest motives of affection. She was in danger.

He knew he couldn't warn her off. He was the last man in the world she would listen to. For all that, he got up and made slowly for a phone box. There was someone inside and he waited impatiently, pacing up and down. At last he got in. He had found her number, begun to dial when his nerve failed him. There was something better he could do than this, something more responsible and adult. As soon as he thought of it, he wondered why he hadn't done it days ago. The green directory then this time.... He took a deep breath and, tapping his fingers nervously on the coin box, waited for Matchdown Park C.I.D. to answer.

Inspector Ulph was a small spare man with a prominent hooky nose and olive skin. David always tried to find counterparts in art for living human beings. He had likened Susan Townsend to Millais' portrait of Effie Ruskin, Magdalene Heller had about her something of a Lely or even a Goya, and this policeman reminded him of portraits he had seen of Mozart. Here was the same sensitive mouth, the look of suffering assuaged by an inner strength, the eyes that could invite and laugh at esoteric jokes. His hair was not as long as Mozart's but it was longer than is usual in a policeman, and when he was a boy it had no doubt been the silky pale brown of the lock David had seen preserved at Salzburg.

For his part, Ulph saw a tall lean young man, intelligent-looking, not particularly handsome, whose eager eyes for a moment took ten years off his age. He poured out an impulsive story and Ulph listened to it, not showing the excitement which the name of North had at first evoked. What had he expected to hear? Not this. Disappointment succeeded his small elation and he stalled, summing his visitor up. Only one sharp pinpoint of his original excitement remained, and he left it glimmering to say briskly:

'You're telling me that Mr North and Mrs Heller have been meeting, to your certain knowledge, at a London public house called The Man in the Iron Mask? Meeting there at regular intervals before her husband and his wife died?'

David nodded emphatically. He had hoped for a sharper reaction than this. 'Yes, I am. It may be far-fetched, but I think they met there to plot, conspire, if you like, to kill the others and make their deaths look like suicide.'

'Indeed?' Ulph's eyebrows had gone up. No one looking at him now would have supposed him to be a man obsessed by thoughts of a gun and a subtly contrived exit. He looked as if David's suspicions, the bare idea that North might be anything but totally innocent, were a revelation to him.

'I'm sure he did it,' David said impulsively, 'and if he did it she must have been in it too. Only she could have told him when Heller would arrive at Braeside and only she could have given him the gun. I visited Heller's flat the night before he died and I saw the gun. Later I saw her go into a cinema. I think North was inside that cinema, waiting for her to hand him the gun in the dark.'

The gun. This was the only way, Ulph thought, that North could have got it. Not by burglary, not by the unimaginable sleight of hand necessary to filching it from Heller himself, but through a conspiracy with Heller's wife. Immediately he saw pitfalls and he said, 'You say North and Mrs Heller first met at this pub in August?'

'Yes, I think it was this way. Bernard Heller had met Mrs North, fallen in love with her, started this affair of theirs, and North found out about it. So he got in touch with Magdalene Heller.' David paused and drew a deep breath. He was beginning to feel proud of himself again. His theory was forming as he spoke and it sounded good to him. 'They arranged to meet and discuss—well, the wrong that was being done them. For a while they didn't do anything more. Bernard tried to commit suicide in September—I read that in the paper—and it must have shaken them. But when he took up with Louise again, they went on with their meetings and decided to kill the others.'

It was so full of holes, so remote from life as Ulph knew it, that he almost laughed. But then he remembered that, absurd as this theory was, a farrago of nonsense, he owed to it the one clue he had as to how North had come into possession of the gun, and he only sighed. The proper study of man is mankind, he thought, and he wondered how anyone as intelligent, as articulate and as alert as this man who confronted him, could have lived nearly thirty years on this earth yet be so blind to man's cautiousness and the pull convention exerts over his conduct.

He said gently, 'Listen to me, Mr Chadwick.' For this, he thought, is going to be quite a long speech. 'An ordinary middle-class quantity surveyor discovers that his wife is unfaithful to him. There are several things he can do. He can discuss it with her; he can discuss it with the man; he can divorce her.' Under the desk he felt his hands begin to clench and he relaxed them. Hadn't he done all these things himself? 'He can do violence to one or both of them, kill her, kill them both. Also he might just contact the wife of his wife's lover and reveal his discovery.

'This last is a possibility. You or I,' Ulph said, 'you or I might not do it, but it has been done. The innocent pair confront the guilty pair. More violence or more discussion follows. What the innocent pair do not do is meet in a pub and plot a murder. Strangers to each other? Knowing nothing of each other's emotions, propensities, characters? Can you hear it? Can you see it?'

Ulph began to speak in a tone quite unlike his natural voice, boyishly, impulsively. Was this North's manner of speech? David had no idea. He had never heard it. ' "We both hate them, Mrs Heller, and want to be rid of them. Suppose we make a foolproof plan to kill them? Suppose we plan it together?" ' But Magdalene's voice he did know and he flinched a little, so uncanny was Ulph's imitation of her long vowels and her sibilants. ' "What a lovely idea, Mr North! Shall I help you work it all out?" '

David smiled in spite of himself. 'Not in those words, of course, but something like that.'

'Wouldn't she have run from him? Called the police? Are you saying that two people, brought together only because their marriage partners were lovers, found in each other a complementary homicidal urge? It says much for your virtue. You've evidently never tried to involve a stranger in a conspiracy.'

But he had. Only two days ago he had attempted just that with Susan Townsend. He had gone to a stranger in the absurd hope she would help him to hunt North down. Why hadn't he learned? Recent experience should have taught him that people don't behave like that.

'Suppose I go back to the pub,' he said diffidently. Was that amusement in Ulph's eyes? 'Suppose I get the names of those two men?'

'As long as you don't get yourself into trouble, Mr Chadwick.'

David walked slowly out of the police station. He felt humiliated, cut down to size by Ulph's expertise. And yet Ulph had only shown him that his reasoning had been at fault. He had done nothing to alter David's conviction of North's guilt or diminish the growing certainty that North was pursuing Susan Townsend to find out how much she knew.

Chapter Fourteen

It was just his luck that Sid and Charles weren't in The Man in the Iron Mask tonight. Perhaps they never came in on Thursdays. He couldn't remember whether he had ever been there on a Thursday himself before. Certainly he couldn't remember any occasion when he had been there and they hadn't. He hung about until eight and then he went home.

On the following night all the regulars were there, the middle-aged couple, the old actor, the girl with the mauve fingernails and her boy-friend, this time wearing a Battle of Waterloo tricorne hat, everyone but Sid and Charles. David waited, watching the clock, the door, and at last he asked the barman.

'Those two bearded characters, d'you mean?'

'That's right,' David said. 'You called them comedians. There's something I wanted to see them about.'

'I doubt if you'll see them in here.' The barman looked at him meaningfully, setting down the glass he had been polishing. 'Keep it under your hat, but I had a bit of a ding-dong with them yesterday lunchtime. Always money, money, money with them it was. Like a disease. The very first time they came in here they started on me about giving wrong change, over-charging, that sort of guff.' He lowered his voice. 'You wouldn't believe the insinuations. Well, yesterday I'd had about enough. Get the police if you're not satisfied, I said. We've nothing to hide. I'm within my rights to refuse to serve you, I said, and if you come back to-morrow I will.'

'The same sort of thing happened to them last August at The Rose,' David said hopelessly.

'I shouldn't be at all surprised. I'm right in thinking they're not friends of yours, aren't I?'

'I don't even know their names.'

'A pub crawl,' said Pamela Pearce. 'Well, I don't know, darling. It could be dreary.'

'There are two chaps I want to find. I've got to find them.'

'I suppose they owe you money.'

'No, they don't,' David said crossly. 'It's much more serious than that, but I'd rather not explain. Come on now, it might be fun having a drink in every pub in Soho.'

'Intoxicating. Still, I don't mind if it's Soho. But, darling, it's pouring with rain!'

'So what? You can wear your new raincoat.'

'That's a thought,' said Pamela, and when he came to pick her up she was glittering in silver crocodile skin.

At Tottenham Court Road tube station he said, 'They've both got beards and their conversation is almost exclusively concerned with money.'

'Is that all you've got to go on?'

He nodded and avoided meeting her eyes. It had occurred to him that Sid and Charles, when at last run to earth, would certainly make cracks about his concern to find a striking-looking dark girl, his ex-secretary. Pamela knew very well he had never had a secretary. Strange that this didn't worry him at all.

They would go first to The Man in the Iron Mask. There was just a chance some of the other regulars might remember North and Magdalene. But David doubted this. He had been a regular too, but he had no recollection of ever having seen the couple—the conspirators? the lovers?—until the inquest day. Did Sid and Charles only remember because like the majority of men they had been susceptible to Magdalene's beauty?

He must find them.

Pamela walked along beside him in silence while the rain fell softly and steadily through grey vapour.

It was Sunday and Julian Townsend was taking his son out for the day. Hand in hand they walked down the path towards the parked car. Susan watched them go, amused because the Airedale who only barked at unknown interlopers, had suddenly begun to roar at Julian. He had become a stranger.

She shrugged and went indoors. In the hall glass her reflection walked to meet her and she stopped to admire herself, the fair hair that had a new gloss on it, the grey eyes alight with happy anticipation, the new suit she had plundered her bank balance to buy. The fee from Miss Willingale could be used to make that good, for she had only four more chapters to complete.

Bob's footsteps sounded in the sideway. No more formal front door calling for him. Susan looked at the mirrored girl and saw in her face pleasure at the new intimacy, the beginning of taking things for granted.

She went to meet him a little shyly. He came in and took her in his arms without a word. His kiss was long, slow, expert, almost shocking in its effect on her. But they were only friends, she told herself, friends in need, each other's comforters. She broke away from him, shaken, unwilling to meet his eyes.

'Bob, I . . . Wait for me a moment. I have to get my gloves, my bag.'

Upstairs the gloves and the bag were ready where she had left them on the dressing table. She sat down heavily on the bed and stared at the sky, hard blue this morning, at the elms that swayed lazily, seeing nothing. Her hands were shaking and she flexed them, trying to control the muscles. Until now she had thought that the year passed without a man, a lover, had been nearly insupportable on account of the lack of companionship and the pain of rejection. Now she knew that as much as this she had missed sexual passion.

He was waiting for her at the foot of the stairs. She remembered how the girl in Harrow had turned to look at him, how Doris had spoken of his looks and his charm, and these opinions, the spoken and unspoken views of other women, seemed suddenly to enhance him even more in her eyes. All but his own wife were overpowered by that physical presence, that quintessence of all that a man should be and should look like. She thought of his wife fleetingly now as she came down towards him. Why had this one woman been impervious, indifferent?

He smiled at her, holding out his hands. There was something shameful in wanting a man because of his looks and because—ugly, shameful thought—you wanted a man. She came closer and this time it was she who put out her arms to him and held her face up to be kissed.

'We'll have lunch,' he said, 'in a little country pub I know. I've always liked little pubs.'

She held his hand, smiling up at him. 'Have you, Bob?'

He said nervously, 'Why did you say it like that? Why do you look like that?'

'I don't know. I didn't mean to.' She didn't know, nor did she know why Heller and Heller's widow had suddenly come into her mind. 'Let's make a pact,' she said quickly, 'not to talk about Heller or Louise while we're out today.'

'God,' he said, and she felt him sigh as briefly he held her against him, 'I don't want to talk about them.' He touched her hair and she trembled a little when she felt his fingers move lightly against her skin. Her relief should have matched his own, but she felt only a vague dismay. Had they anything else to talk about, anything at all in common? There was something painfully humiliating in the thought which had crept into her mind. That instead of going out with him she would have preferred to stay here like this, holding him, touching her cheek to his, in an eternal moment of warmth and of desire. Outside this room they would have, it seemed to her, no existence as a pair, as friends.

The sharp bright air shocked her as if out of a dream. She walked ahead of him to his car and she was appalled at herself, like someone who had committed an indiscretion at a party and now, in the light of day, is afraid to face both his neighbours and his partner in that fall from grace.

Doris looked out of her window and waved. Betty looked up from her gardening to smile at them. It was as if she and Bob were going off on their honeymoon, Susan thought, and the pink cherry petals fell on to her hair and her shoulders like confetti on a bride. She got into the car beside him and then she remembered how harsh he had been with her the day he had driven her to Harrow, violent almost as he drove deliberately fast to frighten her. It was the same man. He smiled at her, lifted her hand and kissed the fingers. But she didn't know him at all, she knew nothing about him.

Whatever she said it would come back to Heller. It always did. But she had promised not to mention him or Louise and now she realised that although Bob himself would do so and derive a strange comfort from the tragedy, he became uneasy if she took the initiative herself. It was as if the double suicide was his private possession that no one, not even she, might uncover and look at without his permission.

The idea was very disagreeable to her. He was thinking about it now. She could see it in his face. For the first time she put into silent words what she had known since that other drive in this car with him. He thought about it all the time, day and night without rest.

She must talk to him about something. 'How are you getting on with Mrs Dring?' she asked desperately.

'All right. It was good of you to persuade her, Susan, sweet of you.'

'She can only come on Saturdays?'

'Yes, when I'm there.' He took one hand from the wheel, touched her arm. Not from desire, she thought, not out of affection. Perhaps simply to assure himself that she was really there. Then he said, his voice very low, as if they were not alone in a car but walking in a crowded street where anyone could hear unless he whispered, 'She talks to me about it. I try to keep away from her, but every chance she can, she talks to me about it.'

'She's rather thoughtless,' Susan said gently.

He set his mouth, but not defiantly. He was controlling the trembling of his lips. 'She opens the windows,' he said.

And thereby let fresh air and sound into the secret thing he kept there? Susan suddenly felt cold in the stuffy car whose heater blew out a hot breeze. In a monotone, low yet rapid, he began to tell her about the questions Mrs Dring had asked him, of her maudlin tactless sympathy.

'I'll have a word with her.'

But he hardly seemed to hear her. Once more he had returned to that morning, to his arrival at Braeside, to the couple on the bed. And, pitying him, not wanting him to know she was also a little afraid, Susan put her hand on his arm and rested it there.

'I couldn't find them,' David said. Ulph's expression was that of an indulgent father listening to a child's tall stories. Perhaps he had never really believed in the existence of Sid and Charles. He made David feel like a crank, one of those people who go to the police with wild accusations because they want to make mischief or attract attention to themselves. And it was on account of this that he said no more of his quest with Pamela Pearce, of their visits to eighteen different pubs, of the perpetually repeated subsequent quarrel when their tempers were frayed by frustration and the incessant rain.

'I should think they work in the City,' he said, feeling foolish. 'We could try the Stock Exchange or Lloyds, or something.'

'Certainly *you* could try, Mr Chadwick.'

'You mean you won't? You wouldn't put a man on it?'

'To what end? Do any of the other regulars at this pub remember seeing Mr North and Mrs Heller there?' David shook his head. 'From what you have told me of their conduct, your two bearded acquaintances aren't remarkable for their probity. Mr Chadwick, can you be sure they weren't—well, having you on?'

This time David nodded stubbornly. Ulph shrugged, tapping his fingers lightly on the desk. He too had much in his mind his professional discretion prevented him from revealing. There was no reason to tell this obstinate man how, since his last visit, North and Mrs Heller had again been separately questioned and had emphatically denied any knowledge of the other prior to the suicides. Ulph believed them. Mrs Heller's brother-in-law and Mrs Heller's neighbours all knew Robert North by now. They knew him as the kind benefactor who had first shown his face in East Mulvihill five days after the tragedy.

And, because of this, Ulph had lost his faith in David's theory as to the gun. He still believed in North's guilt, still had before his eyes that moving picture of North's actions on that Wednesday morning. But he had acquired the gun some other way. Ulph didn't know how, nor did he know how North had got out of the house. Answers to these questions would help him to get the case reopened, not unfounded theories as to a conspiracy.

'You see, Mr Chadwick,' he said patiently, 'not only do you have no real evidence of conspiracy existing, you have no theory to convince me such a conspiracy would be necessary. Mrs Heller offered her husband a divorce when she first discovered his infidelity and only failed to petition because for a time he wanted them to try to keep their marriage going. He couldn't have prevented her divorcing him as the guilty party. It wasn't even as if he tried to conceal the truth from her. He loved Mrs North, was committing adultery with her, and he told his wife so. As to North, he might have committed a crime of passion from jealousy or hurt pride. That's a very different matter from conspiring for months with a comparative stranger. His anger would cool in that time. Why take the enormous risk premeditated murder entails when with all the evidence he had, he too had only to seek a divorce?'

He said no more. Show me, he thought, how this man in the jealousy and the rage I can understand came into possession of a gun he could not have possessed and left a house unseen.

She had invited him often enough and yet, he thought, she would be dismayed to see him. By now North would have told her of his visit to Matchdown Park. He stood on the doorstep for a second or two, hesitating, before he pressed the bell. The red and yellow glare from the neon signs, the passing buses, rippled and flickered on the peeling wall and the chalk graffiti.

It was the brother-in-law who let him into the flat. In the half-dark it might have been Bernard Heller and not Carl on whose face the slow smile dawned, Bernard who stood aside to let him enter.

The flat smelt of greens and gravy. They had shared a meal and the dirty plates were still on the table. Magdalene Heller was standing against the wall underneath the mandoline, an unlighted cigarette in her fingers.

'I thought it was time I looked you up,' David said, and with a sense of rightness, of retribution, of destiny almost, he stepped forward with his lighter. The flame threw violet shadows on her face and her eyes widened. She said nothing for a moment but David felt that she too recalled the parallel forerunner of this scene and had, as he had, a sense of having been there before. He half-expected her to glance quickly over her shoulder, searching for North's face. She sat down, crossing her long beautiful legs.

'How are you getting on?'

'All right.' Her gruffness, her gracelessness almost, reminded him a little of Elizabeth Townsend. But whereas Mrs Townsend's sprang from the confidence born of background, upbringing, connections, Magdalene's was the attitude of a woman sure of her own beauty, of the lily that needs no gilding.

It was Carl who said, 'People have been very kind, Mr North most of all.' David fancied that the girl stiffened a little at the name. 'He's lent Magdalene money to tide her over.' Carl smiled bovinely as if to say, There, what do you think of that? 'More like an old friend,' he said, and when David slightly raised his eyebrows, 'The police even came here and asked Magdalene if she'd known him before.'

David's heart seemed to run a little, to trip. So Ulph *was* interested.... 'But of course she hadn't,' he said innocently.

Magdalene crushed out her cigarette. 'Why don't you put the coffee on, Carl?'

While Bernard's twin lumbered off to do her bidding, she fixed David with those green eyes in which the gold specks, particles of metal dust, moved sluggishly. 'Tell me something.' Her accent was strong tonight. 'Did Bernard ever tell you how he met that woman?'

'He told me nothing,' David said. 'How did they meet?'

'It was last August in Matchdown Park. She was in a friend's house and he came to fit a spare part to the heating. She'd been ill and she had a bad turn so he said he'd drive her home. That was how it started.'

Why are you telling me this? he wondered. The words had been bare, almost all monosyllabic.

'He told me it all,' she said. 'Bob North didn't know a thing. I had to tell him. It's not surprising, is it, we got together after the inquest? We had plenty to tell each other.'

'But the police somehow believe you and North had met before?'

Pure hatred flashed briefly in her eyes. She knew why the police had questioned her and who had alerted them, but she dared not say. 'I never set eyes on Bob till three weeks ago,' she said, and brusquely, tossing her head so that the black hair swept her shoulders. 'I'm not worried. Why should I be?'

'No coffee for me,' David said when Carl came in

with the tray. He had a strong revulsion against eating or drinking anything in this flat and he rose. 'I suppose *Equatair* have given you something?' he said baldly, for there was no longer any question of impertinence or of tact between him and her. The memory of her full pink mouth pressed against his skin sickened him.

'Precious little,' she said.

'I don't suppose it was easy for them getting someone to go to Switzerland in Bernard's place.' David turned to look at Carl. 'Not in your line, I suppose?'

'I speak the language, Mr Chadwick, but, no, I am not clever like Bernard was. I shall go to Switzerland for my usual holiday. I was born there and my relatives are there.'

Magdalene poured her coffee very slowly as if she were afraid her hands would shake and betray her. Suddenly David felt sure he must keep in touch with her brother-in-law. Once before he had failed to secure an address. He nodded to the widow, keeping his hands behind his back, and he met her sullen eyes before following Carl into the hall.

'I may go to Switzerland myself,' he said when they were out of earshot, side by side, almost touching in the narrow passage. 'If I wanted a bit of advice ... well, would you let me have your address?'

Carl's sad face lit with pleasure. He looked a man whose counsel is seldom sought. David gave him a pen and an old envelope on which he wrote in a long sloping hand his address and a landlady's phone number.

'Any time, Mr Chadwick.' He opened the door, peered out. 'I thought we might have the pleasure of seeing Mr North tonight,' he said. 'Once or twice I've been here when he has called to see Magdalene. But he is a busy man and his neighbours take up so much of his time....'"

His neighbours. One neighbour, David thought. He crossed the street and as he slipped the envelope into his pocket his hand touched the card he had bought in the National Gallery. Under a street lamp he stopped to look at it. Was North with her now? Was North making love to her, just as Magdalene Heller had tried to make love to him, David, and for the same reason?

She was very lovely, this girl that Millais had painted, had wrested from Ruskin and had finally married. Susan Townsend was exactly like her, as like as Carl was to Bernard. It might have been her photograph which, bent and a little soiled now, David carried with him in his pocket. He wondered how he would feel if, instead of buying it, he had received it from her as a gift.

At East Mulvihill station he bought his ticket and then, swiftly, before he had time to dwell too much on what he was about to do, he went into a phone box.

Chapter Fifteen

'Mrs Townsend, this is David Chadwick. Please don't ring off.' Did his voice sound as intense to her as it seemed to him? 'I wanted to talk to you. I couldn't just leave things.'

'Well?' It could be a warm word, a word denoting health or things excellently done, but she made it the coldest in the world. On her lips it as onomatopoeic, a well indeed, a place of deep, dark and icy waters.

'I haven't phoned to talk of—what I mentioned to you last week. I don't intend to discuss Mr North.'

'That's good, because I wouldn't discuss him.' She was neither scathing nor hectoring. It was hard to say what she was. Iron-firm, implacable, remote.

'It was appalling what I did last week and I apologise profoundly. Can you understand when I say I want to see you and explain that I'm not a lout or a practical joker? Mrs Townsend, would you have dinner with me?'

Unable to see her, he couldn't define the atmosphere of her silence. Then she said, but not scornfully, *'Of course not,'* and she laughed. In her laughter he detected neither mockery nor outrage. She wasn't even amused. She was incredulous.

'Lunch, then,' he persisted. 'In some big crowded restaurant where I couldn't—couldn't frighten you.'

'I was frightened.'

In that moment he fell in love with her. Until then it had been a silly dream. Why had he been such a fool as to telephone and create for himself in five minutes a load of sorrow?

'I was frightened,' she said again, 'because I was alone and it was dark.' Again the silence fell and the pips sounded, remote, careless of what they terminated. He had his coin ready, his breathless question.

'Are you still there?'

Her voice was brisk now. 'This is rather a ridiculous conversation, don't you think? I expect you acted in good faith and it doesn't matter now, anyway. But we don't really know each other at all and the only thing we could talk about—well, I wouldn't talk about it.'

'It isn't the only thing,' he said fiercely. 'I can think of a hundred things just offhand like that.'

'Good-bye, Mr Chadwick.'

He went down the escalator and when he was alone in the passage that led to the platform he dropped the picture card to be trampled underfoot in the morning rush.

She was almost sure Bob hadn't overheard that conversation, but when she returned to the living-room he lifted his eyes and they had a haunted look. Should she lie to him, tell him it was someone the agent had put on to her, a prospective buyer of the house?

'I heard,' he said. 'It was that fellow Chadwick.'

'Only to ask me out to dinner,' she said soothingly. 'I shan't go. Of course, I shan't.'

'What does he want, Susan? What's he getting at?'

'Nothing. Don't, Bob, you're hurting me.' His hands which were so soft when they stroked her cheek, seemed to crush the bones in her wrists. 'Sit down. You were saying, before he phoned . . . ?'

The hard fingers relaxed. 'About Louise,' he said. 'I was telling you how she and Heller met and how he drove her home. Magdalene Heller's told me the whole story. After that they used to meet when I had to work late.' His voice was feverish, desperate. 'In cafes, in pubs. He got in such a state he tried to kill himself. I wish to God he'd succeeded then. He started writing those horrible letters to her . . . Susan, you *did* burn those letters, didn't you?'

She was past caring now whether she told the truth to him or lied. What, anyway, was the truth? 'I burnt them, Bob.'

'Why can't I forget it all, put it behind me? You think I'm going mad. Yes, you do, Susan, I can see it in your face.'

She put her head in her hands, running her fingers through her hair. 'Keep away from Mrs Heller, if she upsets you,' she said presently. 'You've done enough for her.'

'What d'you mean?'

'You've given her money, haven't you?'

He sighed and he sounded infinitely weary. 'I'd like to get away, go far away. Oh, Susan, if only I didn't have to go back to that house tonight! Or ever again to see Magdalene Heller.' He paused and said as if he were stating something profound, yet at the same time novel and appalling, 'I don't ever want to see Magdalene Heller again.'

'Nor me, Bob?' Susan asked gently.

'You? It would have been better if I'd never met you, never seen you . . .' He got up and his face was as white and strained as if he were ill or really demented. 'I love you, Susan.' His arms went round her and, his lips almost touching hers, he said, 'One day, when I'm—when I'm better and all this is past, will you marry me?'

'I don't know,' she said blankly, but she kissed him on a long sigh and it seemed to her that no kiss had ever been so pleasurable and so sweet. 'It isn't the time yet, is it?' she said as their mouths parted and she looked up into that strained haunted face.

'There's the boy, I know,' he said urgently, reading her thoughts. 'He's frightened of me. That'll pass. We could all go away, couldn't we? Away from Mrs Dring and this Chadwick and—and Mrs Heller.'

The play for which David had designed the sets ended and the credit titles came up. He thought he might as well watch the news. The first item was the result of some West Country by-election which interested him not at all and he had got up to turn it off when he stopped, intrigued by the voice of a speaker who had suddenly replaced the announcer. That lilting intonation, those stressed r's were familiar. He had heard them before that evening on the lips of Magdalene Heller. Her accent, far less strong than that of the commentator, had always puzzled him and now he located it at last. She came from Devon.

Immediately he remembered the newspaper picture of Robert and Louise North. That had been taken in Devon while they were holidaying there last year. Did it mean anything or nothing?

Very carefully he repeated in his mind the conversation he had had with Magdalene two hours before and it seemed strange to him that she had taken such pains to tell him how her husband and Louise North had met. Because the circumstances of that meeting caused her real distress, or because in fact they had not met that way at all? Of course it was possible that Bernard had driven her home because she was unwell, had promised perhaps to enquire after her subsequently, and that from this beginning their love affair had grown. But wasn't it far more likely that they had all met on holiday?

Once more David felt excitement stir. Suppose they had met, the two couples, in an hotel or on a beach? Then, when Louise and Bernard returned respectively to Matchdown Park and East Mulvihill, intending to follow up the attraction which had already begun, the last thing they would have done was talk to friends or neighbours of this apparently brief holiday acquaintance. But North and Magdalene would have a knowledge of each other, a shared memory which, however casual, would make their later meetings natural.

In this case North might well have contacted Magdalene to disclose his wife's conduct, or Magdalene him to reveal Bernard's. Even Ulph, David thought, wouldn't find anything fantastic in such a supposition.

He hesitated for a moment and then he dialled Carl Heller's number. The landlady answered. Mr Heller had just come home from his sister-in-law's, he was taking off his coat at this moment. The telephone slightly distorted his voice, making it more guttural.

'There is nothing wrong, I hope, Mr Chadwick?'

'No, no,' David said. 'It was just that I thought of going to Switzerland for a few days at Easter and it occurred to me you might be able to recommend somewhere to stay.'

Carl began to reel off a list of names and places. He sounded almost animated, over-helpful, as Bernard had been when asked favours. And David recalled how this man's dead brother, when asked tentatively for the loan of a fireplace, had pressed on him not one but a dozen of the latest models. Thus Carl, instead of naming a couple of *pensions*, selected from his memory hotels and tourist centres in every Swiss canton, pausing only for David to make, or pretend to make, copious notes.

'That'll do fine,' David said when Carl drew breath. 'I suppose your brother and his wife often stayed at this one?' And he named a modest hotel at Meiringen.

'My brother never went back to Switzerland after he was married. He was trying, he told me, to become like an Englishman and he dropped all his continental ways. He and Magdalene had their holidays in England, in Devon where Magdalene comes from.'

'Really?'

'That is why I was so pleased for them, for the Zürich appointment. Wait till you see real mountains, I said to Magdalene. But then my brother does this wicked thing and ...' Carl's heavy sigh vibrated through the earpiece. 'It is a funny thing, Mr Chadwick, it will amuse you, although in a way it is sad. Always in Devon they are staying in the same place at Bathcombe Ferrers, and the place they stay at, it is a small *pension* called—what do you think?—the Swiss Chalet. Often my brother and I have laughed about this. But you are a great traveller, I know, and would not be content with such a place. No, you must go to Brunnen or maybe Lucerne. Mount Pilatus now—you have it on your list like I have told you? You have the name. ...'

In his hand David had only the soiled envelope on which Carl had written his address and now, feeling a little ashamed of the deceit he had practised, he wrote beside it just five words.

Chapter Sixteen

A rustic sign with its name burnt on in poker-work informed him that he had arrived. Nothing else gave a clue as to why this place had been named 'The Swiss Chalet'. It was an Edwardian house, three storeys high with scarcely any visible roof. A superabundance of drain-pipes, tangled like creeper, climbed all over its façade.

The entrance was through a conservatory full of pots and Busy Lizzie. David opened the inner glass door and found himself in a hall that in colour and decoration might have been the subject of a nineteenth-century sepia photograph. He approached a cubby-hole in the wall which reminded him of a ticket office window at an almost totally disused station. On its shelf stood a bell, a brass bell painted with edelweiss and the name

Lucerne. Honour was satisfied. In the Swiss Chalet there was at least one genuinely Swiss object.

Its shrill-throated ring brought a little round woman from a door marked Private. David stuck his head through the aperture, wondering if this was how it had felt to be put in the stocks. The woman advanced aggressively upon him as if she might at any moment throw a rotten egg or a tomato.

'Chadwick,' he said hastily. 'From London. I booked a room.'

The threatening look faded but she didn't smile. He put her age at just over sixty. Her hair was dyed to the shade of coconut matting, which it also resembled in texture, and she wore a mauve knitted twinset, a miracle of cable stitch and bobbles and loops.

'Pleased to meet you,' she said. 'It's Mrs Spiller you talked to on the phone.' She wasn't a native. Retired here perhaps in the hope of making a fortune. He glanced at the pitch-pine woodwork in need of revarnishing, the lamp in its bakelite shade, the visitors' book she pushed towards him whose emptiness told of failure. 'Room number eight.' He put out his hand for the key. Outrage settled in a crease on her purplish forehead. 'We don't have no keys,' she said. 'You can bolt your door if you're particular. Breakfast's at eight sharp, dinner at one and I do a high tea at six.' David picked up his suitcase. 'Up two flights.' She bobbed out from under a hinged flap. 'The first door on your left. The lav's in the bathroom, so don't hang about washing too long. There's such a thing as consideration.'

Consideration for whom? he wondered. The season had scarcely begun and the place seemed dead. It was ten past eleven, but Mrs Spiller seemed to have forgotten her last exhortation, for as he mounted the stairs, she bellowed after him:

'You never said who recommended me.'

'A friend,' David said. 'A Mrs Heller.'

'Not little Mag?'

'Mrs Magdalene Heller. That's right.'

'Well, why didn't you say so before?'

Because he had thought he must come round to it subtly, with cunning and by degrees.

'You *are* a dark horse. I bet you'd never have said if I hadn't asked. I read all about her tragedy in the papers. It upset me properly, I can tell you. I've got the kettle on. Would you like a cuppa before you turn in? That's right. You leave them bags and I'll get my boy to take them up.'

Things were going well, far better than he had expected. There was one question he must ask. Her answer would make the difference between his staying the whole weekend or leaving in the morning. 'Of course, she was here only last year, wasn't she?'

'That's right, in July. End of July. Now you pop into the lounge and make yourself comfy.'

The room was small and shabby. It smelt of geranium leaves and fly spray. Mrs Spiller shut the door on him and went off to fetch the tea. Sitting down, he wondered how often Magdalene had sat in the same chair. Suppose the Norths had stayed here too and the first encounter between Bernard and Louise had been in this very room? He contemplated the decor with his critical designer's eye, the potted plants, the wedding group on an upright piano, the snowstorm in a glass dome. Two pictures faced him, a water colour of Plymouth Hoe and a nasty little lithograph of some central European city. There was another picture in the corner, half hidden by a mahogany plant stand. He got up to look more closely and his heart gave a little jerk. What more suited to this mid-Victorian room than Millais' *Order of Release?* Susan Townsend looked through him and beyond, her mouth tilted, her eyes cool, distant, indifferent.

Before driving down here, he had done a strange, perhaps a foolish, thing. He had sent her a dozen white roses. Would she look like that when she received them, her expression changing from cold politeness as she closed the door to disgust?

'Sugar?' said Mrs Spiller into his right ear.

He jumped, almost knocking the teacup out of her hand.

'Bit nervy, aren't you? A couple of days down here will set you up. Very bracing, Bathcombe is.'

'It always does Magdalene a world of good,' David said.

'Just as well. You need your health to face up to what she's been through. What a terrible thing, him doing himself in like that, wasn't it? I've often asked myself what was at the back of it all.' Not as often as he had, David thought, sipping the hot sweet tea. 'You being their friend, you must know what triggered it all off. You needn't mind telling me. I'm not exaggerating when I say I was more or less one of the family. Year after year Mr Chant used to bring little Mag here for their holidays and Mag always called me Auntie Vi.'

'Still does,' David said stoutly. 'She often talks about her Auntie Vi.' But who was Mr Chant? Her father, of course. In the newspaper bundling his slide projector had been the announcement of Heller's wedding, Bernard Heller to Miss Magdalene Chant.

'Yes,' said Mrs Spiller, reminiscing, 'she'd been coming here with her dad since she was so high and she knows all the locals. Ask anyone in the village if they remember little Mag Chant pushing her dad about in his wheelchair. Well, not his. They used to borrow one from old Mr Lilybeer and she'd take him down to the beach. Her and Bernard, they came here for their honeymoon and then most years after that.'

'I don't suppose that Mrs North ever stopped here?'

'North?' Mrs Spiller considered and her face reddened. 'Are you referring to that woman as was Bernard's fancy piece, by any chance?' David nodded. 'She certainly did not. Whatever gave you that idea?'

'Nothing really,' David began.

'I should think not indeed. He must have been out of his mind chasing a woman like that when he had a lovely girl of his own. All the local boys was after Mag when she was in her teens, or would have been if her father'd given them half a chance.'

'I can imagine,' David said soothingly, but he was aware that for the time being at least he had spoiled the hopeful *rapport* between himself and Mrs Spiller. She was staunchly Magdalene's ally, as if she were really her aunt, and she took his introduction of Louise North's name as criticism of this adopted niece, of her beauty, her desirability. 'I think Magdalene's exceptionally good-looking.'

But Mrs Spiller was not to be so easily mollified. 'I'm off up the wooden hill,' she said and she gave him an aggrieved frown. 'You can have the telly on if you want.'

'A bit cold for that.' The room was unheated and a vaseful of wax flowers had been placed in the grate.

'I never light no fires after April the first,' said Mrs Spiller sharply.

He had discovered one thing. The Norths had not only not stayed at the Swiss Chalet at the same time as Bernard and Magdalene. They had never stayed there at all. But they had been better off than the Hellers and perhaps they had stayed at one of the hotels in the village.

David breakfasted alone off cornflakes, eggs and bacon and very pale thick toast. He had finished and was leaving the dining-room when the only other residents appeared, a dour-looking man and a middle-aged woman in tight trousers. The woman eyed David silently while helping herself from the sideboard to four bottles of different kinds of sauce.

It was a cool cloudy morning, sunless and still. He found a path between pines which brought him within ten minutes to the top of a cliff. The sea was calm, grey and with a silver sheen. Between two headlands he saw a pointed heathy island rising out of the sea and he identified it from Turner's painting as the Mewstone. This association of nature with art again evoked Susan Townsend's face, and it was in a depressed frame of mind that he set off for the village.

At the Great Western Hotel he ordered morning

coffee and was shown into a wintry lounge. The place was as yet barely prepared for visitors. Through a large curved bay window he could see a one-man manually-punted ferry that plied between the Bathcombe shore and a tiny beach on the opposite side.

'A friend of mine, a Mr North,' he said to the waitress who came for the bill, 'stayed here at the end of July last year, and when he heard I was coming down he asked me if I'd enquire about a book he left in his room.'

'He's left it a long time,' said the girl pertly.

'He wouldn't have bothered only he knew I was coming down.'

'And what would this said book be called?'

'*Sesame and Lilies*,' said David because he kept thinking of Susan Townsend who was Ruskin's wife all over again. With what he thought must be a mad smile, he left all his change from a ten shilling note on his plate.

'I will enquire,' said the girl more pleasantly.

David watched the ferryman come to the Bathcombe shore. He unloaded a cargo of empty squash bottles in a crate. Possibly the single cottage on the other side was a guesthouse. Come to that, the Norths could have rented a cottage here or a flat or stayed with friends. They might not have come in July, they might not have come to this part of Devon at all.

The girl came back, looking sour. 'Your friend didn't leave that gardening book of his here,' she said. 'He didn't even stay here. I've checked with the register. You'd better try the Palace or the Rock.'

But the Norths hadn't stayed at either place. David crossed the inlet by the ferry to find that the solitary house was a youth hostel.

Shepherd's pie and queen of puddings was served at the Swiss Chalet for luncheon. 'Well, did you meet anyone who knows Mag?' asked Mrs Spiller when she came in to serve him instant coffee and pre-sliced processed cheese.

'I hardly saw a soul.'

The coconut matting curls bounced and all the bobbles on the lilac jumper quivered. 'If it's excitement you want, I don't know why you didn't settle for Plymouth. Folks come to Bathcombe to get a bit of peace.'

Suppose the Norths had 'settled for' Plymouth? They might have come to Bathcombe just once for a day's outing. But would a passionate love affair have arisen from one isolated encounter on a beach? David couldn't picture slow, stolid Bernard, his deck-chair moved alongside Louise's, exchanging addresses surreptitiously.

'I'm not complaining,' he lied. 'It's a charming place.'

Mrs Spiller sat down and put her fat mauve elbows on the table.

'That's what Mr Chant always used to say. "It's a charming place, Mrs Spiller. You get real peace and quiet here," he'd say, and him coming from Exeter where it's not what you'd call rowdy, is it? By the way, I've been meaning to ask you, how's Auntie Agnes?'

'Auntie Agnes?'

'I'd have thought Mag would mention *her*. Not that you could blame Mag, a bit of a kid like her, but I've always thought she had a lot to thank Auntie Agnes for. But for her she never would have gone to London and got married.'

His mind wandering, David remarked that perhaps this wouldn't have been a bad thing.

'You've got something there.' Mrs Spiller passed him Marie biscuits from a packet. 'But she didn't know how it was all going to turn out, did she? I remember back in 1960 thinking to myself, that poor kid, she'll never have a proper life tied to an old man like that.'

'Mr Chant, you mean?' David said absently.

'Well, maybe I shouldn't call him old. I dare say he wasn't above fifty-five. But you know how it is with invalids. You always think of them as old, especially when they're crippled like Mr Chant was.'

'Arthritis or something, was it?'

'No, you've got it wrong there. Multiple sclerosis, that Auntie Agnes told me. She came down with them in 1960 and he was real bad then. Too much for Mag on her own.'

'I suppose so.' David wanted to get on with the hunt. He wasn't interested in diseases of the central nervous system and he was awaiting his chance to escape from Mrs Spiller.

'They're very slow in developing, them illnesses,' she was saying. 'You can have sclerosis for twenty or thirty years. Mind you, he had his good days. Sometimes he has nearly as good as you or me. But other times . . . It went right to my heart, I can tell you, watching that lovely girl pushing him about in a chair and her only in her teens.'

'Her mother was dead by then, I suppose?' David said, bored.

'That's what they used to tell people.' Mrs Spiller put her face closer to his and lowered her voice. The middle-aged couple sat some fifteen feet from them, looking out of the window, but Mrs Spiller's extreme caution implied that they were spies whose sole mission in visiting her guesthouse was to satisfy themselves as to certain unsolved mysteries in the Chants' family history. 'I got it all out of that Auntie Agnes,' she whispered. 'Mrs Chant had run off with someone when Mag was a kid. They never knew where she ended up. Saw what her life would be, I reckon, and got out when the going was good.'

'Like Magdalene.'

'A wife's one thing,' Mrs Spiller bristled. 'A daughter's quite another. When Auntie Agnes wrote and said Mag was going up to London to find herself a job I thought, that's the best thing that could happen. Let her have a bit of life while she's young enough to enjoy it, I thought. Of course, Auntie Agnes wasn't young, her being Mr Chant's own auntie really, and it's no joke looking after an invalid when you're past seventy.'

'No doubt she managed.'

'I don't reckon she looked ahead when she took it

on. She wasn't to know Mag'd meet Bernard and write home she was getting engaged. Mind you, I never knew any of this till Mag and Bernard came down for their honeymoon. That was two years later and Mr Chant had passed on by then. That's why I asked if you knew what had become of Auntie Agnes. Dead and gone too, I dare say. It happens to all of us in the fullness of time, doesn't it?'

'Depends what you mean by the fullness of time,' said David and he thought of Bernard with a bullet through his head because he had loved unwisely.

Susan had begun on the last chapter of *Foetid Flesh* when Bob opened the back door and came in softly. She stopped typing at once, a little dismayed at the look on Paul's face. He had been trundling his cars between the legs of her chair, but now he squatted still and stiff and his expression would have seemed a mere blank to anyone but his mother who could read it.

'Where did the flowers come from, Susan?'

It was Paul who answered him. 'A man called David Chadwick. Roses are the most expensive thing you can send anyone in April.'

'I see.' Bob stood with his back to them, staring out of the window at the elms on which not a bud, not a vestige of green, showed. 'Chadwick ... And daffodils are the cheapest, aren't they?'

'You picked your daffodils out of the garden.'

'All right, Paul. That's enough,' Susan said. 'It's not so long ago you said it was silly to send people flowers.' She smiled at Bob's back. 'And you were quite right,' she said firmly. 'I can see Richard outside. I expect he's wondering where you are.'

'Then why doesn't he call for me?' But Paul went, dodging the hand which Bob suddenly and pathetically put out to him. Susan took it instead and, standing beside him, again felt the physical pull he exerted over her, the attraction that emptied her mind and left her weary.

'Have you thought about what I asked you?'

For a moment her only answer was to press more tightly the hand she held. And then it came to her in a swift unpleasant revelation that this was her reply. Physical contact and then renewed stronger physical contact was the only way she could get through to him. The closer intimacy which awaited them if they married would be just this pressure of hands on a full and complete scale, the desperate soulless coupling of two creatures in a desert.

She looked up at him. 'It's too soon, Bob.' His face was grey and drawn, no longer even handsome, and it was tenderness rather than desire that made her want to kiss him. She moved away, for suddenly her delaying answer had made kissing wrong. 'Come and sit down,' she said. 'You don't mind about the roses, do you? I don't know why he sent them.'

'Because he wants to know you better, of course. Susan, the world is full of men who'll want to know you better. That's why I have to—you have to ... Susan, if I'd seen you as I see you now, when Louise was still alive, would you have ... ?'

'When Louise was alive?'

'If I'd fallen in love with you then, would you have come away with me?'

She was afraid without knowing the reason for her fear. 'Of course I wouldn't, Bob. Even if you'd wanted to marry me then, Louise couldn't have divorced you. She was a Catholic.'

'My God,' he shouted, 'I know that!'

'Then, don't torment yourself.' She hesitated and said, 'I suppose you could have divorced her.' And would it have been different, would there have been true companionship for them without the spectre of Louise's death and Heller's between them, their sole wearisome topic of conversation? 'Yes, you could have done that,' she said tiredly.

'But I couldn't have done that,' he said, and his eyes had darkened from blue to a frightening impenetrable black. 'It's because I couldn't have done that ... Oh, Susan, what's the use? It's past, gone for ever. Heller

loved my wife and killed her and I ought to be free . . .
Susan, I'll never be free!' He quieted, shivered, and
gradually his face assumed the look it wore when he
explored his obsession. 'Everyone persecutes me,' he
said. 'The police have been here again. Didn't you hear
that dog? The whole street must have seen.'

'But why, Bob?'

'I suppose your friend Chadwick put them on to
me.' There was a sneer on the fine-drawn mouth as he
glanced at the white roses. 'They wanted to know if I'd
known Magdalene Heller last August.' He turned to
stare at her with those sombre eyes and she, meeting
them, was for the first time afraid of him. 'She persecutes me, too,' he said in a dull dead voice.

Susan said helplessly, 'I don't understand.'

'God knows, I hope you never will. Then there's
your Mrs Dring.' He drew in his breath sharply. 'I gave
her the sack this morning. It was bad enough having to
listen to her going on about Louise, but I could have
stuck that.'

'What happened, Bob?'

'I found her rooting through Louise's dressing table.
I think she was looking for those letters. She must have
read about them in the papers and thought she'd got
the chance of a peepshow. There was a scene, I said
things I shouldn't have and so did she. I'm sorry,
Susan. Nothing goes right for me, does it?'

He put out his hand to her very slowly as if to pull
her towards him, and she was on her feet, bewildered
and uneasy, moving to clasp that outstretched hand,
when the telephone rang urgently into their silence. He
dropped his head into his hands with a gasp of despair.

Susan lifted the receiver and sat down heavily when
she heard Julian's brittle chit-chat voice.

'I've found a buyer for the house, my dear. Our old
friend Greg.'

Knowing him of old, Susan sensed that the pause
had been made for her to fill with praise and congratu-
lation. Like someone hazarding a half-learned foreign
language, she felt the must speak just to prove she

could. Anything she might say would do. 'Why does he want to live out here?'

'You may well ask,' Julian said, 'after that delicious little mews place of his. The fact is Dian has been playing up and he feels there are too many naughty temptations in London. So I'll send him along, shall I?'

'I hope I'll still recognise him.'

She was aware that Julian had made some sharp sarcastic reply to this, but the words were just words, meaningless, without power. At the sound of a movement from the living-room, she looked up and saw Bob framed in the doorway. His face and body were in shadow, a dark silhouette, and, poised there, his figure suggested a man on the brink of an abyss. She covered the mouthpiece with her hand.

'Bob . . .'

He made a queer little gesture with one of those shadowed hands as if staving something off. Then he moved out of her sight and she heard the door to the garden close.

'Are you still there, Susan?'

'Yes, I . . .' How different this conversation with Julian would have been if she could have used it as the opportunity to tell him she was going to be married! In that moment she knew quite certainly she could never marry Bob. 'I'll see Greg any time he likes to come,' she said calmly, and then, with the politeness of a distant business acquaintance, 'It was good of you to phone. Good-bye.'

She sat by the phone for a long time, thinking how she and Bob were separated now only by two thin walls and ten feet of air. But those barriers were as impenetrable to her as the enclosures of his mind. She shivered a little because when they kissed or sat in silence she was almost happy with a happiness quenched at once by glimpses into that hooded mind.

Chapter Seventeen

Using his story of the lost book, David spent Saturday afternoon calling at every hotel on the South Devon coast between Plymouth and Salcombe and at each he drew a blank. Plymouth itself defeated him. He counted twelve hotels and guesthouses in the A.A. guide alone and, having tried four of them, he gave up. The Norths must have rented a house or stayed inland.

Must have? The chances were that they had been to North Devon, that they had been there in May or June. And Magdalene might have been telling the truth. It was not on a beach or a seafront restaurant that Bernard had met Louise but in fact in a suburban kitchen, drinking tea.

'Had a good day?' asked Mrs Spiller, slapping a plateful of pork pie and lettuce in front of him. 'Pity it's too early in the year for you to do the boat trip to Plymouth. But they don't run till May. Mag always went on them boats. Still, I dare say you wouldn't fancy it, you being the nervy type.'

He had never thought of himself as a neurotic. Perhaps the urgency and at the same time the fruitlessness of his quest was telling on him. 'Is it a particularly perilous voyage?' he asked sarcastically.

'Safe as houses normally, only there was the *Ocean Maid,* after all, wasn't there?'

The name rang a faint bell and then he vaguely recalled distasteful headlines and remembered reading in the papers of a catastrophe, similiar to the *Darlwyne* tragedy, but with a happier ending. A glance at Mrs Spiller told him she was avid for conversation and he had no one else to talk to, nothing to do. 'She was a pleasure boat,' he said. 'Didn't she go aground off the coast here?'

Mrs Spiller took a cup from a side table and filled it

from David's teapot. 'She was taking folks on trips from Torquay and Plymouth, calling in here and at Newton. Due back at six she was. The next thing we knew it was on the wireless she was missing.' A few drops of tea fell on to her embossed lilac bosom. She took a paper napkin from a tumbler and scrubbed at the stain. 'Drat that tea! What was I saying? Oh, yes, well, Mag had been a bit bored and lonely, not knowing what to do with herself, so I said, Why not go on the boat trip? and she did. I got her a real nice packed lunch and I saw her off on the boat myself, never thinking they'd go and run out of fuel and get themselves stranded overnight.

'Just a pair of slacks and one of them thin tee shirts she had on. You've got a lovely figure, so why not show it off? I said. Mighty cold she must have got on that boat, though. Well, it got to six and it got to seven and still she hadn't come and then we heard about it on the news. I was in a proper state, on the point of sending a wire to Bernard. You don't know what to do in a case like that, do you? You don't know whether you're worrying them needlessly like. Especially as I'd egged Mag on to go, got her ticket and all. I blamed myself really.'

'Didn't he go on the trip, then?' David put his knife and fork down and looked up, suddenly chilled.

'Go on the trip? How could he? He was up in London.'

'But I thought you said . . .'

'You're miles away tonight, Mr Chadwick, you really are. This was *last* year, last July. Mag came down on her own. You're mixing it up in your mind with the other years when Bernard came with her. Anyway, as I said, I never wired him and it was all right and poor little Mag none the worse for what she'd been through. She didn't let it keep her in for the rest of the time she was here. Palled up with some folks she'd met on the boat, she told me, and she was off with them every day. I was glad I hadn't got Bernard down here all for nothing, I can tell you. You've gone quite white, Mr Chadwick. Not feeling queer, I hope?'

Magdalene hadn't lied. Bernard had met Louise just as she had told him. Perhaps it was true also that she had never set eyes on North until the inquest, had never plotted with him to do a murder, never handed him a gun nor sat with him in The Man in the Iron Mask. Wasn't it possible too that Sid and Charles had never seen them there together, but had concocted an amusing story to while away half an hour while they drank the drinks he had paid for?

On Sunday morning he packed his case and left the Swiss Chalet. Five miles inland he stopped for petrol in a village called Jillerton.

'Clean your windscreen, sir?'

'Thanks, and would you check the tyre pressures while you're about it?'

'Can you hang on five minutes while I see to this gentleman?'

David nodded and strolled across the village street. One day, he thought, he might look back to this weekend and laugh at himself. It had taken him a two-hundred-mile drive and surely two hundred questions besides two wasted days to find out that Bernard Heller had never been here at all.

There was only one shop in the street and, although it was Sunday, the door was open. David went inside aimlessly, eyeing the coloured car stickers, the pixie statuettes and the carved wooden stags, replicas of which he had seen for sale in Vienna, in Lacock, in Edinburgh and on the pavement by Oxford Circus underground. On a shelf behind this array of mass-produced bric-a-brac stood mugs and jugs in Devon pottery, hand-painted in cream and brown and not unattractive. He could think of no one but Susan Townsend to whom he wanted to give a present and if he bought her a souvenir she would probably send it back. The white roses might be wilting on his doorstep at this moment.

Some of the pottery was lettered with obscure proverbs and this he disregarded, but the mugs, plain and prettily shaped, had a christian name written on each of them, Peter, Jeremy, Anne, Susan ... There would have to be one for Susan, of course. What was wrong with him, what sentimental madness had seized him, that everywhere he looked he had to see her name or her face?

There was a plain one at the end of the shelf that he could buy his mother for her nightly hot chocolate. He lifted it, turned it round and saw that it wasn't plain after all. In common with the rest it had a name written in elegant brown calligraphy.

Magdalene.

Could Bernard have ordered it for Magdalene on one of those previous visits of theirs, ordered it and neglected to collect it? He was setting it down again thoughtfully when a voice behind him said, 'A very uncommon name, isn't it, sir?' David turned in the direction from which the deep Devon burr had come and saw an assistant who was perhaps his own age. 'I've often said to my wife, we'll never sell that one, not with a name like Magdalene.' And, raising his voice, he called to someone in the room behind the shop, 'I'm saying to this gentleman, we'll never sell that mug Mr North ordered.'

'Mr North?'

'I remember because the circumstances were a bit—well, funny,' said the assistant. 'Last August it was, right in the height of the holiday season. Still, you won't want to be troubled with that, sir. The gentleman won't come back for it now, so if you're interested ... But no, not with a name like Magdalene.'

'I'll have it,' David said in a bemused voice.

'I call that handsome of you, sir. Ten and sixpence, if you please.'

'You said there were funny circumstances.'

Wrapping-paper in hand, the young man paused. 'If you're going to have it, I reckon you're entitled to know. The gentleman was staying at the King's Arms. That's the inn on the far side of the green and my uncle keeps it. Mr North ordered the mug for his wife, he said, but when he didn't come for it and he didn't come I had a word with uncle. 'Tis a Mrs *Louise* North, he says, not Magdalene. Queer that, we thought. Looks as if 'twere for a lady friend and the gentleman not quite above board.'

'So you didn't want to embarrass him by taking the mug over to the hotel?'

'Proper embarrassing it would have been too, sir, seeing as the lady, his true wife that is, fell sick with one of these here old viruses the day after they came. 'Twould have set her back a bit to hear her husband was carrying on.'

'Is the King's Arms that smart-looking pub on the green, did you say?'

'That's it, sir.'

North had a fondness for smart little pubs. . . .

'Rather unfortunate for them, Mrs North being ill like that,' David said casually and, as he spoke, he remembered Magdalene Heller's words. When Bernard met her she had been ill. . . . So it was after this holiday, then, they had met? 'It must have spoilt their time here.'

'Mr North didn't let it get him down, sir.' The assistant shrugged, perhaps at the villainy of mankind in general or London people in particular. 'Went on that boat trip, he did, without his wife. The *Ocean Maid,* you'll have read of in the London papers. He told me the tale when he came in to order that little mug, how they'd been drifting for hours, never knowing how close they were to the rocks. 'Twould put you or me off our holiday properly, wouldn't it, sir? But that Mr North, he didn't turn a hair. I said to my wife at the time, you can see it's take a mighty big upheaval to get him down.'

Susan was almost sorry she was nearing the end of *Foetid Flesh.* In a way it had taken her mind off the tragedy next door and off Bob. Now her problems, only subconsciously present while she typed, would rush to fill the hours the finishing of the typescript must leave empty.

Page four hundred and two. The whole thing was going to run into four hundred and ten pages. Jane Willingale's handwriting had begun to deteriorate in the last fifty sheets and even to Susan, who was used to it, some words were nearly indecipherable. She was trying to interpret something that looked like an obscure shorthand outline when Doris hammered on the back door and walked in with Richard.

'You don't mind if I leave him with you for a bit, do you, my dear? Just while we go for drinks with the O'Donnells. Bob was asked but he won't go anywhere these days. If you ask me, he's got persecution mania. Still, you'll know more about what goes on in his mind than the rest of us, no doubt. The police were here for hours in the week. Did you see?'

'Bob told me.'

'And I heard him yelling at your Mrs Dring when I was passing yesterday. He's in a very nasty nervous state. Many a time I've seen them like that in the nerve wards. I expect you know best, but if I were you I shouldn't fancy being alone with him. White roses, I see. They'll soon wilt up in this temperature. Unlike me. I could stay here all day, but I can see you want to get on. Pity it's always so perishing at the O'Donnells'.'

The outline was 'murder'. Susan typed it with a faint feeling of inexplicable distress. She heard Richard go upstairs and the sound of little cars trundled out on to the landing. Seven more pages to go. To decipher the last, almost hysterical rush, of Miss Willingale's novel was going to demand all Susan's concentration.

The children had moved their toys to the stairs now. She must be tolerant, she must control the admonition until they became really unbearable. Bump, bump, crash, whirr.... That was the latest tank plummeting to make a fresh dent in the hall parquet.

'You're making an awful racket,' she called. 'Can't you go outside for a bit?'

'It's raining outside,' Paul's voice came indignantly.

'You know you're not to play on the stairs, anyway.'

She waded through a long sentence and turned the page. The writing had suddenly improved.

My darling,
    You are in my thoughts night and day. Indeed, I do not know where dreaming ends and . . .

It didn't make sense. But this wasn't even Jane Willingale's writing. It sloped more, the capitals were larger, the ink different.

Susan frowned and, taking a cigarette, inhaled deeply. Then, holding the sheets up to the light, she contemplated Bernard Heller's love-letters.

Chapter Eighteen

'Can we take the motorway outside?' Paul asked, adding virtuously, 'It's stopped raining, but the grass is wet and I thought I ought to ask you.'

Susan hardly heard him. 'What, darling?'

'Can we take the motorway outside?'

'The electricity won't work outside and it's too cold to leave the door open.'

Paul stuck out his lower lip. 'It's not fair. We can't play on the stairs and we can't come in here because you're working. You've got your papers in an awful mess again and you've got ash all over them. If I mess them up you just get mad.'

So she had never burnt the letters. Perhaps in her heart she had always known she hadn't, but she also knew that she had certainly not tucked them between the main body of Miss Willingale's manuscript and the penultimate page. What reason would Doris have for doing such a thing, Doris or Mrs Dring?

'Paul, you haven't been playing with my papers again, have you?'

'No, I haven't!'

'Are you quite sure?'

'I haven't touched them,' the little boy flared. 'I *swear* I haven't. Cross my heart. I haven't been at your desk since the day before you were ill, the day you had to go to the trial about Mrs North.' Self-righteous indignation turned his face a bright tear-threatening red. 'You said if I touched them again you wouldn't let me wear my watch and I didn't touch them.'

'You needn't make a big thing out of it. I believe you.'

'Except for once,' he said defiantly, 'the day you were first ill. I wanted to *help*. Your papers were in an awful mess. You'd left some of them on the coffee table so I put them back with the others, all tidy. I thought you'd be pleased!'

David was jubilant. He had been right, he hadn't wasted his time. Beyond all doubt now, Robert North and Magdalene Heller had known each other since last summer.

He was jubilant, but there was much he didn't understand. All along he had assumed that their meeting, knowledge of each other, love perhaps for each other had grown from the love affair between their marriage partners. Now it seemed that these two, the widow and widower, had met first. North had gone alone on a boat trip and when it seemed they would be stranded at sea all night had been drawn towards Magdalene who was very likely the only other passenger on that holiday voyage. David could picture her, a little frightened perhaps, but still flaunting her body in her trousers and her thin tee shirt, and he could picture North comforting her, lending her his coat.

But Bernard had been in London and Louise ill in bed.

Was it credible that on returning home North or
Magdalene had brought the four of them together?
Hardly, David thought. North had ordered the piece of
pottery for her, had surely met her every day for the
rest of his holiday. Mrs Spiller had spoken to him of
her having 'palled up' with someone she met on the
boat. By the end of their holiday, David was sure, they
were already in love. North would never have introduced Magdalene to his wife nor she North to her husband.

How, then, had they contrived that the others should
meet?

David spent Monday morning in Knightsbridge
among the antique shops, hunting for Chippendale furniture to dress the set of *Mansfield Park*. His search
was fruitful and at half past twelve he crossed the
street to the tube entrance on the corner of Hans Cres-
cent.

A girl whose face seemed familiar came out of
Harrods at that moment and bore down on him relentlessly. Recognition came with a sickening twist. It
was ironical that he should encounter the second Mrs
Townsend when more than anything in the world he
wanted to see the first. The absurd coincidence made
him smile and she took the smile as an enthusiastic
greeting.

With a violent snort, she dumped an enormous
coloured paper carrier on the pavement between them.
'So you didn't buy that place, then?' she said with the
loud directness he found repellent. 'Did you know Greg
was after it? Only he won't cough up more than eight
thou and God knows we're on our beam ends. There's
wads of it going out every month to that woman in
Matchdown Park and what's left all goes on nosh.' She
drew breath noisily. 'You wouldn't believe what I've
just had to pay for a lobster.'

David eyed her warily. She looked younger than
ever this morning and particularly uncouth. The one-
piece garment she wore—a dress? a coat?—was made
of thick oatmeal-coloured material, striped here and

there with grey and fringed at hem and wrists. It made her look like a squaw, the juvenile delinquent of the tribe.

'My husband is bonkers about food,' she said. 'Here, you might as well carry that for me. It weighs a ton.'

In fact, it must have weighed close on half a hundredweight. As David lifted the bag, a protruding bundling of wrapping paper slipped and a large red claw sprang out. Elizabeth Townsend marched to the pavement edge.

'Can I get you a taxi?'

'You're joking. I'm going on the bus.' She glared at him. 'D'you know what I'm going to have for my lunch? Yoghourt. That's what I've come down to. And I love food, I just love it.' She sighed and said crossly, 'Oh, come on, before the lights change.'

He followed her, humping the bag.

'I thought I might go to lunch with Dian,' she said petulantly. He almost asked who Dian was and then he remembered the mews house and the flaming bamboo screen.

'Why don't you? It's only just down the road.'

'Well, I don't quite like to. I'm not usually funny about these things. Julian says I rush in where angels and all that jazz. No, the point is Dian's got a man giving her a whirl. Not really like Dian, is it?'

David said heartily that indeed it was not.

'I'd have said Dian was the complete prude. Frigid, I expect. But then Minta rang up this morning and when I said I'd drop in on Dian, she said, I wouldn't because her boy-friend's there again.' Thrusting back the red claw, David said he saw what she meant. 'I don't want to burst in on them, you see. For Christ's sake, don't say a word to Dian. I know she's a mate of yours. Live and let live, after all. Dian hasn't said anything to Minta—she wouldn't, would she?'

'I shouldn't think so.'

'But with Minta living opposite she couldn't expect to get away with it. Minta told me this bloke's car's been there half a dozen times in the past fortnight and she's seen him sneaking in after Greg's gone to the studio. Of course, she dropped a hint to Greg and that's why he wants to take Dian out of harm's way.'

Every step was taking him further and further from the tube station. As Elizabeth Townsend trailed relentlessly on past bus stops, he had been searching for an excuse to dump the shopping and make his getaway. And now he did dump it, but not because he wanted to escape.

'Is that all Minta has to go on?" he asked, trying to keep the breathlessness from his voice. 'Just seeing a man's car outside Dian's?'

'She saw him go in,' said Elizabeth Townsend sharply.

'But, Mrs Townsend . . .'

'Oh, call me Elizabeth. You make me feel about ninety-six.'

'But, Elizabeth . . .' It was a relief. The other name conjured up a very different face and voice. 'He could be a salesman, a surveyor, an interior decorator, anything.'

'Yeah? I tell you he's a sexy fellow of thirty and Dian's a real dish. You know damn' well Dian and Greg haven't been having it for two years now and Dian's always off on her own. You can take it from me, she's all mixed-up over this bloke. You're green, David, that's your problem. But Minta's not and I'm not and when we hear a fellow's been sneaking round to a girl when her old man's nicely out of the way, we know what to think.'

'Faithful Dian? Frigid Dian?'

'You are rooting for her, aren't you? So she's not faithful, she's not frigid. This proves it.'

At this point the bottom fell out of the bag. He looked at the aubergines, the lemons and the tins of *fois gras* which rolled into the gutter and said happily, 'Elizabeth, I'm awfully glad I met you. Tell me, if you could choose, what's the nicest place you can think of for lunch? The place you'd most like to go to?'

'The *Écu de France*,' she said promptly, stuffing two

lemons into the pocket of her Red Indian garment and eyeing him optimistically.

'I can't bear to think of you eating yoghourt,' he said. 'I never liked it.' He hailed a taxi and, opening the door, bowled vegetables and fruit and cans on to the seat. 'Jermyn Street,' he said to the driver. 'The *Écu de France.*'

He heard a chair shift and scrape from inside the office as he approached the door and when he came in the woman who was waiting for him sat a yard or two from his desk, her expression grimly virtuous. Ulph was sure she had been examining the papers which lay face-upwards on his blotter. They were a draft of the programme for the police sports gala and Ulph smiled to himself.

'Good morning,' he said. 'You wanted to see me?'

'I don't care who I see,' the woman said, 'as long as it's someone high up, someone as knows the ropes.' She patted her fuzzy red hair with a hand in a Fair Isle glove and she looked at him in truculent disappointment as if she had expected to see someone big, aggressive, authoritative. 'You'll do,' she said. 'I reckon you'd be interested in a fellow called North.'

'May I have your name, madam?'

'As long as it doesn't go no further. Mrs Dring. Mrs Leonard Dring. My first name's Iris.' She took off her gloves and laid them on the desk beside her handbag. 'I work for this North, cleaning like, or I did till he give me the push Saturday. What I wanted to tell you was, I work next door too and I was working there the morning Mrs North was done in.'

Ulph nodded, his face reserved. This was not the first time he had encountered the spite of the discarded servant. 'Go on, please.'

'There was three fellows digging up the road at the bottom of them gardens. Mrs North used to give them their tea, regular like. Well, about nine-thirty it was, I was in Mrs Townsend's kitchenette and I heard this banging on the back door next door. Well, I didn't

think no more about it and I was doing my windows,
in the lounge that is, when I see this chap go down the
garden path, tall chap in a duffel coat. Mrs Townsend
and me, we thought it was one of them workmen. He
lets himself out of the gate and goes off up the road.'

'Perhaps to get his tea at a café instead?'

'So we thought at the time. I reckon that's what he
wanted us to think. The point is there wasn't never
more than *three* men working on the road. I'll tell you
how I know. I said to my husband, How many chaps
was there working on the cemetery road? And he says,
Three. Never more than three. And he's never wrong,
my husband, there's nothing that man doesn't know. I
said, You're pally with that old fellow, the foreman
that was, you ask him. And that's what he did. Three
fellows there was, all the time, the old chap, the man
and the young lad. And what's more, when I heard the
banging at the door that dog never barked. It was out
the front, laying in wait, and it could see the side door
all right. Like my husband always says, them animals
have got more sense than we have. They don't take no
account of duffel coats and folks setting themselves up
as workmen.'

'You delayed a long time before you came to me,
Mrs Dring,' Ulph said quietly. 'Could it be that you've
only come now because you have a grudge against Mr
North?'

'If you don't believe me, you ask Mrs Townsend.
She knows. It was her put the idea into my head.'

Probably she supposed that her departure would be the
signal for him immediately to set the law in motion.
Ulph sat quite still, reflecting. His own construction of
the murder scene, almost totally visual, had shifted and
changed. North had done it very simply, after all. Ulph
saw that there had been scarcely any premeditation at
all and North, who had acted on impulse, had merely
covered his tracks afterwards.

He had stayed at home that morning not to contrive
a false suicide but to have it all out with Heller. He

would have told Louise and let her warn her lover if she liked. Ulph touched his forehead and felt the muscle that jumped above his eye when he was nervous. Hadn't he done just that thing, confronting his own wife and the man she loved? Hadn't he too tried to discuss matters with them rationally and calmly? His wife had shut herself in her bedroom, flinging herself on the bed in a storm of tears.

Very likely it had been that way with Louise North, and the two men had gone up to her together. But first Heller had slung his raincoat and his heavy briefcase on the kitchen table; keeping the gun in his jacket pocket. Ulph knew very well that if a man, even a peaceful, mild man, owns a gun he is liable to use it under stress. Louise had given Heller the idea, perhaps erroneous, perhaps true, that her husband was violent and tyrannical. Aware of the kind of scene which awaited him, Heller would have brought his gun. Just as a threat, of course, just as a tool of persuasion.

And North? Perhaps Heller had arrived later than expected and the husband, tired of waiting, was ready for work in coat and gloves. Thus they had entered the bedroom together. Had they struggled and the gun gone off? Ulph thought so. In the struggle Louise had been inadvertently shot by Heller and when, in his horror at what he had done, he had bent over her, fallen beside her on the bed, North had taken the gun and shot him as he lay. Taken it in a hand already, but perhaps not with murderous intent, protected by a strong driving glove. Then, later, the instinctive actions of self-preservation, Heller's hand to be closed for the second time round the gun—lest the glove had eradicated earlier prints—and, hideously, a third shot to be fired. It had been raining. A duffel coat with hood up, the moment's pause to knock at the back door as the workmen always knocked, and then the deliberately slow stroll, heart pounding, blood thundering to the fence, the street, the wide unsuspecting world outside.

With a good counsel, Ulph thought, North might not get very long. He had been intolerably provoked. The woman had turned his home into a house of assignation and written foul things of him to her lover. And suddenly Ulph remembered how North had spoken of his neighbour's kindness to him, as if he thought of her as more than just a doer of good deeds. She was divorced, he recalled. Was there a chance that she would wait for North?

Ulph got up and cursed himself for a sentimental fool. There had been no woman waiting for him when at last he had found himself a free man. He glanced at his watch. North would be still at work, home in three hours or so. As he prepared the things he must say and do, he thought with a faint amusement of David Chadwick and the theories born of a fruitful imagination. What else could you expect of a scene designer? Still, for a day or two Ulph also had believed in the possibility of collusion, of conspiracy. He felt a little ashamed of himself.

Chapter Nineteen

He looked again at the photograph of the Norths that had been taken on their holiday and this time the background to their smiling faces was familiar. The inn sign was too blurred for its name to be readable, but he recognised the half-timbering on the gables of the King's Arms and the white fence that surrounded Jillerton's village green.

David had stacked this paper with other souvenirs, depressing, a little macabre, of Bernard Heller. Here were the records of his brief and humble intrusions into the public eye, and here the announcement of his marriage to the girl who had wheeled her sick father along the Bathcombe shore. The print was faded but Bernard's handwriting not at all, the figures of his wedding date sharp and blue with the little distinctive and very continental tick across the ascender of the seven.

He looked at them all musingly for a moment and then he went to the telephone. Inspector Ulph was out and no one could tell him when he expected to return. David hesitated, pushed away inhibition and the fear of a rebuff, and dialled again. It was the child who answered.

'May I speak to your mother?'

He sounded a nice sensible boy, older than the impression David had from a fair head once seen on a pillow. 'Who shall I say?'

'David Chadwick.'

'We've got your flowers in a vase.' He could never know how much pleasure he had caused with that simple statement. 'Wait a minute and I'll fetch her.'

David would have waited all night.

'Thank you for the flowers,' she said. 'I was going to write to you, only things—well, haven't been very easy.'

He had meant to be gentle, tactful, cunning in his approach. The sound of her voice stunned him into abruptness. 'I must see you this evening. Can I come now?'

'But, why?'

'I have to see you. Oh, I know you can't stand me and, I tell you frankly, it's North I want to talk about. Don't put the receiver down. I should still come.'

'You're an extraordinary man, aren't you?' There was no laughter in her voice. 'I wouldn't be frightened this time,' she said, and then, 'Perhaps it would clear the air.'

Paul fell asleep quickly that night and Susan wondered if it was because the house was almost certainly sold now. It was still daylight, the evening soft and spring-like, and she had no need of a coat to go next door.

The Braeside windows were all tightly closed. A secret shuttered house, she thought. Hadn't someone once likened death to a secret house? And she forced her eyes not to look upwards as she made her way to the back door.

Bob had taken upon himself the right to enter her house without knocking and, although until now she had never availed herself of it, she felt that with him she must have a similar privilege. This was the first time she had entered Braeside since that Wednesday morning. The door yielded to a push and the kitchen yawned emptily at her. Did it seem bare because Heller's coat and briefcase were missing from the table?

'Bob?'

She had called his dead wife's name like that and, getting no answer, had gone upstairs. Suppose history had repeated itself? The niche where the Madonna had stood was empty now, an open mouth in the wall.

'Bob?'

The living-room was stuffy, but clean and as tidy as if no one had lived in it for a long time. For a second she didn't see him, he was sitting so still in the chair where she too had sat and talked to the police inspector. A bar of sunlight made a wavering gold band down the length of his body, passing across his eyes, but he stared through it, undazzled, like a blind man.

She went over to him, knelt at his feet and took his hands. The touch of his skin was no more exciting to her now than Paul's, and she felt for him only as she sometimes felt for Paul, pity, tenderness and above all an inability to understand. But she loved Paul. Had she ever been close enough to Bob to love him?

'Susan, I've come to the end,' he said. 'The police came to me today at work, but never mind that. Never mind that now. I went mad, I was corrupted, I suppose. I don't want to blame anyone else. If I was led into things—well, I was a grown man and I don't want to blame anyone else.' He held her hands more tightly. 'I'm glad,' he said, 'that they can't get anyone else for all this. They can't find out. You don't know what I mean, do you?'

She shook her head.

'Just as well. I don't want you to know. Tell me, did you ever think I might, well, do you an injury?'

Speechless, she looked at him.

'The suggestion was made,' he said hoarsely, 'and I—for a while I ... It was only for a day or two, Susan. I didn't know what you knew and what you'd seen. I really love you. I love you, Susan.'

'I know,' she said. 'I know.'

'And Louise loved Heller, didn't she? You know that. Everyone knows that.' He gasped and, leaning forward so that the beam of light shivered and cut across his shoulder, said fiercely, 'What I did, it was from jealousy. I couldn't stand ... I had provocation, didn't I, Susan? And maybe I won't have to go away for very long, I'll come back to you.' He took her face in his hands. 'Do you know what I'm trying to tell you?'

'I think so,' she faltered and she stayed where she was, kneeling, because she thought that if she got up she might fall. She had come here to tell him that she still had his wife's letters, that they had never been burnt. His hands palpated her skin. She had thought of him as a blind man but now he was like someone who is deaf and who can only discern speech by feeling the subtle and tiny movements of the speaker's bones.

Perhaps he had really become deaf, for he gave no sign that he had heard the dog begin to bark, hollowly at first and then with fury as the the car door slammed.

'You've been crying,' David said.

'Yes, I didn't know it showed.'

The traces of tears were not disfiguring, only the evidence of an unbearable vulnerability. The puffiness they gave to her eyes, like some beautician's exclusive treatment, served to make her look very young. 'I was boorish on the phone,' he said. 'I'm always boorish with you.'

'It doesn't matter,' she said indifferently. 'At the moment I can't feel that anything much matters. You came to talk to me about—about someone we both know. I think you're too late. I—I don't think he'll come back here.'

'Do you mean he's been arrested?'

'That's what you wanted, isn't it?' she said harshly. He couldn't tell if it was personal hatred in her eyes or despair at the world she lived in. She turned away her head and sat down as if she must, as if her legs would no longer support her. 'Oh, I don't condone it,' she said. 'It's too soon yet, I can't fully realise it.' She swept back the fair hair which had tumbled across her forehead. 'But, d'you know what jealousy is? Have you ever known it? Have you?'

David didn't answer that. 'Is that what he told you?' he asked. 'That he did it from jealousy?'

'Of course.' Her voice was hard and brittle. 'He went over the edge. It was an impulse, he wasn't sane.'

'You're so wrong, Susan.' She had let the christian name pass. From indifference, he thought bitterly. 'I want to tell you something. It might comfort you. I don't say it would make you feel differently towards North, although . . .' He sighed quickly. 'But it might make you think better of me. May I tell you?'

'If you like. I haven't anything else to do. It will pass the time.'

He had wanted very much to tell this story of his, and he would have told it to Ulph had the inspector not been otherwise occupied. It was a dreadful story and, as the truth of it had come to him by degrees during the day, he had shocked himself into a kind of horror. In a way it was as if he had invented it, as a writer of the macabre invents, and then is troubled by the sick fecundity of his own mind. But David knew that his story was true and therefore inescapable. Because it was true and it changed the whole aspect of North's conduct and North's motives, it had to be told. But this girl was the wrong audience, although to him she was right in every other respect. He already felt for her the tenderness that wants to save its object from cruel disillusionment, but it had come to him too that she might contemplate waiting for North and, during that long wait, arrive at what she now denied, condonation of an act that to her was the outcome of uncontrollable jealousy.

'North met Magdalene Heller on holiday in Devon last July,' he began. 'They fell in love. It might be better to call it a physical enslavement on North's part.' She wasn't looking at him and her face was impassive. 'When they came home,' he said, 'they began meeting, sometimes in a London pub and, no doubt, in other places as well. Magdalene wanted him because he's handsome and well-off by her standards. I've told you why he wanted her. Perhaps he also wanted children, but I don't know.' He watched her make a very faint movement of one hand. 'I think it was Magdalene who thought of the idea, who was perhaps, to put it dramatically, North's evil genius. Magdalene had a gun, you see, and in September Magdalene's husband had tried to gas himself because he knew she no longer loved him. A man who attempts suicide may attempt it again and may succeed.

'I don't know when they first began to plan it. Perhaps not until after Christmas. It would have been in January or February that Magdalene gave North one of Heller's business reply cards to hand to Louise and propose that they have central heating installed. No, it wasn't a coincidence that Heller happened to work in the Matchdown Park area. It was because he did that Magdalene formed their plan on these particular lines.'

'What lines?' she said in a low, scarcely audible voice.

'As soon as Louise had filled in the card and signed it,' he went on, 'she began to tell her neighbours about the central heating project. Heller came alone in his car to discuss it with her and every time he came that dog barked so that everyone was aware of his visits. Louise North had been looking very unhappy because she too knew that her husband was being unfaithful to her. She talked to no one of it, but she couldn't help the misery that showed in her face. She had only one thing to distract her, the plan for improving the heating of her house, and of course she told her neighbors about it. But when North was asked by them for his opinion on the scheme, he simply denied all knowledge of it. For this was the one sure way of making certain that Heller's visits would be taken as illicit.'

Now, at last, she did turn her eyes to his. 'But that is quite absurd.' Indignation had replaced all the deadening effect of shock. 'Of course people asked Bob about his central heating and of course he denied it. He told a friend of mine quite decidedly that he couldn't afford central heating. This idea of yours—I don't know what you're leading up to—this idea is ridiculous. If Bob had been lying, what do you suppose would have happened if people had asked him and Louise about it when they were together? Very probably they did ask.'

'And if they did?' David asked quietly. 'Wouldn't it have made them believe all the more firmly in Louise's guilt to hear her insist while her husband turned away and looked embarrassed? Wouldn't they have felt sorry for him as the deceived husband doing everything he could to conceal his wife's treachery?'

'Louise North was in love with Heller,' she said stubbornly. 'He came here three or four times and Bob knew very well why he was coming. Look, I know you're obsessed with these ideas of yours, but you weren't living here. You don't know the people involved. The day before she died Louise came in here in tears to tell me all about it, to beg me to go in there the next day and hear the whole story.'

For a moment he was checked. Suppose his theory was all wrong, all hot imagination? Susan Townsend would never speak to him again. 'She actually told you,' he said urgently, 'that she was in love with Heller?'

A flicker of doubt creased the skin between her eyebrows. 'No, but I . . . Of course she came for that. Why else would she have come?'

'Perhaps to tell you that her husband was being unfaithful to her and to ask your advice.'

She looked at him blankly and then she blushed, deeply and painfully. 'You mean that I would have been a good adviser because my husband had been unfaithful to me?'

It was dreadful that he, of all people, should have to wound her in this way. His throat was dry and for a moment he couldn't speak. Then he said, 'Because of that, of what you said, she wouldn't have expected you to show much sympathy to the guilty partner of a marriage, would she? And yet that is what you believed she was.'

'I still believe it,' she said with sudden passion. 'I believe in Bob's unhappiness.'

'Yes, I expect he was unhappy. There can't be much happiness in being driven to do frightful acts by a woman like Magdalene Heller. They flared at each other at the inquest, didn't they? All acting, or perhaps the rage of Lady Macbeth?'

'What are you really trying to say?'

'That Bernard Heller and Louise North weren't lovers at all. That they were never more to each other than salesman and housewife.'

Chapter Twenty

She took a cigarette and lit it before he could. Her hands were very steady. The puffiness under her eyes had almost gone, leaving blue shadows. He noticed how thin her hands were, so thin that the wedding ring slid to the first joint when she moved her fingers.

He stammered a little. 'You've taken it very calmly. I'm glad of that.'

'Only because I know it isn't true.'

He sighed, but not with exasperation. How could he expect her to understand inconstancy, disloyalty? 'I know it's hard to take at first,' he said quietly.

'Oh, no, it isn't that.' Her face was almost serene. 'When you began I was afraid it was all going to be true, and now I know it isn't I feel, well, easier. I don't bear you any malice,' she said seriously. 'I know you meant to do the right thing. I like that.' She gave him a stiff brisk smile. 'You're a kind considerate person, really. It's true that . . .' And now she lowered her eyes. 'It's true that I let myself get fond of Bob North. We needed comfort from each other very much because . . .' Her voice had grown very matter-of-fact, 'Because we'd reached a low ebb in our lives. I'm getting over the shock of it now. I'm used to shocks,' she said. 'He did a dreadful thing and we shall never see each other again. It wasn't as if we really ever had much in common. I'm going to move away quite soon and I've always got my little boy to think of. I shall never forget Bob, how frightened he was and how haunted.' She paused and cleared her throat. 'But you want to know why I'm so sure your idea's wrong.'

'Yes,' he said tiredly, 'yes.'

'Well, then. Heller and Louise were in love, I know they were. You see, Heller was writing love-letters to Louise as far back as last November. I've got them here—Bob left them with me—and you can see them if you like.'

'Forged,' David said, as he turned them over in his hands, although he knew they couldn't be. He had remembered them now, letters which had been identified in court by Magdalene and by *Equatair*'s managing director and by Bernard's own brother. 'No, I know they can't be.' He read them while she, lighting a second cigarette from the first, watched him with gentle sadness.

'You see, they're both dated 1967, last year.'

He read them again, slowly and carefully, and he looked again at the dates, November 6th, '67, and December 2nd, '67. There was no doubt when they had been written, but there was something wrong with them just the same. "He is not an old man and may live for years. He has no rights, no hold over you that anyone would recognise these days."

'How old is North?' he asked.

'I don't know,' she said and she stopped, distress puckering her face. 'About thirty, in his early thirties.'

'Odd,' David said. 'Strange that Heller should have described him like that.'

'But it's true, he isn't an old man.'

'No, he's so young that it was absurd of anyone who knew his age to write of him like that. That's the way you talk of someone in late middle-age, someone of, say, fifty-five. It's as if Heller were arguing with someone very young, putting the maturer, more realistic viewpoint. And what about this? "We just have to hang on and wait till he dies." Why should North have died? He's strong and healthy, isn't he, as well as young? And that about his rights, about him having no rights that anyone would recognise these days. I should think ninety per cent of the population wouldn't deny that husbands and wives have legal and moral rights over each other, and the hold is pretty strong.'

'It takes a good deal of legal machinery to break it,' she said dryly. 'But you're forgetting that Heller was in an unstable state, he was writing hysterically.'

'And yet these letters aren't hysterical. Parts of them are calm and tender. May I ask why North gave them to you?'

'He wanted them burnt. He hadn't the strength of will to do it himself.'

David almost laughed. The man had wanted them burnt all right because although on first glance, on cursory examination, they seemed genuine, a closer perusal might have shown some oddity that revealed Louise could not have been their recipient. Why had he shown them to Susan Townsend? Because he wanted to be sure of her sympathy, her pity, her recognition of himself as injured. He had succeeded, David thought bitterly.

'Do you know what I think?' She didn't, she didn't seem to want to. She was listening to him out of politeness. He went on just the same. 'I believe the man referred to wasn't a husband at all. The woman who received these letters was tied to someone, certainly, but tied only by duty.' He looked up and saw that she was very tired. 'Forgive me,' he said. 'May I take these letters away with me?'

'I don't see why you shouldn't. No one else wants them.'

She gave him her hand, passed before him into the hall. It was as if he had called to see her on some practical business, as if he and not the society photographer had bought her house.

'You shouldn't be alone,' he said impulsively. 'I wouldn't leave you, only you must loathe the sight of me.'

'Of course I don't, but I'm quite used to being alone. I was in a bad state after the inquest, but I was ill then.' She opened the front door and as soon as he appeared, framed in light, the dog began to howl. No wonder North had stroked its head, patted it, that last night David had been here, for it had been his innocent henchman. 'I wish we could have met under different circumstances,' she said.

'But we have met.' He didn't wait for her answer, for it might have quenched hope.

Until she was married Magdalene Heller had lived with her father, a victim of multiple sclerosis, then aged about fifty-five. She had been a devoted nurse to him until she went to London and met Bernard. But she couldn't get married and leave her father; she had to wait for him to die. Mr Chant must have needed a great deal of care and attention that could only be provided by the daughter who understood. The chronic invalid was harsh and ungrateful, resenting the health of the girl who nursed him and sometimes violent to her. But it was her duty to stay with him and see her fiancé only occasionally, when he could come and stay near her in Exeter or she manage a day in London.

David assembled these facts in his mind and when he came to East Mulvihill he had formed a theory, subsidiary to his first, like the tiny offshoot on the body of a hydra. Carl Heller opened the door of the flat to him. Did Magdalene retain him there like a porter to do her bidding? His dull lethargic face was abject to-night, the heavy jowls as pendulous as a bloodhound's.

'You have seen the morning papers?' he asked, pausing between each guttural word. 'They have arrested Mr North for killing my brother.' Never before had David seen anyone actually wring his hands. 'Oh, my brother and his wrongdoing . . .' He seized David's arm with a quick clumsy movement. 'I can't believe it. Magdalene is sick, lying down. Yesterday when he did not come and he did not phone I thought she would go mad.' He shook his head, threw up his hands. 'She is better now, calmer. And all this misery has come upon us through my brother's wrongdoing.'

'I don't believe he did anything wrong, Mr Heller. He wrote some letters once to Mrs North, didn't he?'

'Wicked letters. I shall never forget how in the court I had to say those letters were written by my brother to that woman.'

'But he did write them to her?' David followed him into the sitting-room. The table was bare and the place tidy, but every piece of furniture was filmed with two days' dust.

Carl sat down, but jumped up again immediately and began to lumber about the room like a carthorse in a stall made for a pony. 'I don't mean he did not write them,' he said, 'but that I was ashamed to say he had. My brother to write of poor Mr North that he was useless and better dead!'

'Mr Heller . . .' David knew that it would be pointless to try to explain to this man whose slow stupidity was intensified because he was distraught. 'Will you tell me something? It may be meaningless to you, not to the point at all, but tell me, how did Bernard make his sevens?'

Astonishment, anger even, at the apparent inconsequence of the question wrinkled Carl's brow while his face—did he think David was mocking righteous chagrin?—flushed a dull brick red. But he stopped pacing and, taking the pencil David handed to him, licking the tip of it, drew a seven with a tick across the ascender.

'I thought so. He was educated in Europe, in Switzerland. Now make a one the way Bernard did.'

For a moment it seemed as if Carl wouldn't comply. The frown deepening, he stared at David, and then, shrugging, drew on the paper an outline very like an English seven. David slid the paper from under the big hand and looked at it thoughtfully. Magdalene had married Bernard in 1962, had met him in 1961. It all fitted and yet ... Why hadn't the police seen who had access to Bernard's current notebooks, why hadn't the managing director of *Equatair* who knew Bernard's writing and style of making figures, why hadn't Carl?

'You said to me once that for the sake of getting on in his job, Bernard wanted to appear as English as possible. Did he ever alter his way of making these continental ones and sevens?'

'I think he may have.' Carl nodded, not understanding, not wanting to understand. 'Five years ago he said to me he would make himself so English no one would know.'

David said softly, 'Five years ago, then, he began to write his sevens without the tick and his ones as an upright stroke ...' He said it softly because he had heard a door open behind him and footsteps in the narrow passage.

She was in a dressing-gown. A negligée would have been wrong for her and the thing she wore was a long stiff bell of quilted stuff, black shot through with blood red. It caught the light like armour. Her face was white and stiff and quite old-looking. She was a queen on a court card, the queen of spades.

'Back again?' she said. She was trying to be defiant but she was too frightened to manage the strong voice necessary for defiance. 'I want a drink of water,' she said to Carl. He fetched it, nodding humbly. Her nails rattled against the glass and she spilled some of the water. It trickled down her chin and on to the black quilting. Now she had a voice again, a poor travesty of a voice, as if she had really aged. 'Bob North killed them, after all. Just as well we didn't have any more to do with him. He must have been a fool, letting himself get caught like that.'

'Murderers ought to be caught,' said Carl stupidly.

'They ought to be tough,' she said, 'and see they don't.'

'I wonder if you would be tough enough,' David said, and he added conversationally as he got up, 'It would be interesting to see.' It will be interesting, he thought, tonight, or tomorrow. The green eyes, iridescent, shallow, rested on him for a long moment, and then she went back into the bedroom, the glass in her hand, her long stiff skirts rustling on the floor. He listened as he passed the door but behind it there was only a silence so deep as to be stronger and more frightening than any sound.

'I wanted to know,' David said when she answered the phone, 'if you were all right.'

'But you phoned last night to know that,' she protested, 'and again this morning.' At least, he thought, she didn't say, 'Back again?' 'I'm quite all right. Really I am. Only the police are here all the time . . .'

'I want to see them myself, but afterwards, may I come and see you?'

'If you like,' she said. 'If you like, David.' She had called him by his name and his heart turned a little. 'But no stories, no theories. I couldn't stand any more.'

'I promise,' he said. She would have to attend the trial and by then she would know him well enough to let him go with her. She would hear it all there and she would need him beside her when she heard the evidence against the two people in the dock.

So David put the phone down and went to tell Ulph what Magdalene Heller and Robert North had done. How they had invented a love affair between two mild and gentle people who had never harmed them except by existing; how they had spread upon their characters so much filth that her friends and neighbours and his twin brother had vilified them; how they had done it simply because Louise North could not divorce her husband and Heller was going to take his wife away to Switzerland.

But before he went into the station entrance, he paused for a moment and leaned against the railings of the treeless park. They had driven past this place, he and Bernard Heller, and yet it was not as he had been then that David suddenly saw him, nor as he had been when he lay dead in the arms of the dead woman he had never really known. He remembered instead the fat jovial clown and the tedious jokes and the unfailing generous kindness.

Perhaps he would tell Ulph of his last discovery first. He was not a vindictive man, but he wanted to see Ulph's face when he learned that Magdalene Heller had kept her own love-letters, the letters Bernard had sent her in 1961, and used them as documentary evidence of an adultery that had never been. He wanted to see Ulph's expression and, ultimately, that of a judge and a jury.